PENGUIN POPULAR CLASSICS

OTHELLO
BY WILLIAM SHAKESPEARE

D0806489

PENGUIN POPULAR CLASSICS

OTHELLO

WILLIAM SHAKESPEARE

PENGUIN BOOKS

PENGUIN BOOKS

Published by the Penguin Group
Penguin Books Ltd, 80 Strand, London WC2R ORL, England
Penguin Putnam Inc., 375 Hudson Street, New York, New York 10014, USA
Penguin Books Australia Ltd, Ringwood, Victoria, Australia
Penguin Books Canada Ltd, 10 Alcorn Avenue, Toronto, Ontario, Canada M4V 3B2
Penguin Books India (P) Ltd, 11 Community Centre, Panchsheel Park,
New Delhi – 110 017, India
Penguin Books (NZ) Ltd, Cnr Rosedale and Airborne Roads, Albany, Auckland,
New Zealand
Penguin Books (South Africa) (Pty) Ltd, 24 Sturdee Avenue, Rosebank 2196, South Africa

Penguin Books Ltd, Registered Offices: 80 Strand, London WC2R ORL, England

www.penguin.com

Published in Penguin Popular Classics 1994
Reprinted with line numbers inserted 2001
19

Copyright 1936, 1955 by the Estate of G. B. Harrison

Printed in England by Cox & Wyman Ltd, Reading, Berkshire

Except in the United States of America, this book is sold subject
to the condition that it shall not, by way of trade or otherwise, be lent,
re-sold, hired out, or otherwise circulated without the publisher's
prior consent in any form of binding or cover other than that in
which it is published and without a similar condition including this
condition being imposed on the subsequent purchaser

CONTENTS

THE WORKS OF SHAKESPEARE

APPROXIMATE DATE	PLAYS	FIRST PRINTED
Before 1594	HENRY VI *three parts*	*Folio* 1623
	RICHARD III	1597
	TITUS ANDRONICUS	1594
	LOVE'S LABOUR'S LOST	1598
	THE TWO GENTLEMEN OF VERONA	*Folio*
	THE COMEDY OF ERRORS	*Folio*
	THE TAMING OF THE SHREW	*Folio*
1594–1597	ROMEO AND JULIET (*pirated* 1597)	1599
	A MIDSUMMER NIGHT'S DREAM	1600
	RICHARD II	1597
	KING JOHN	*Folio*
	THE MERCHANT OF VENICE	1600
1597–1600	HENRY IV *part i*	1598
	HENRY IV *part ii*	1600
	HENRY V (*pirated* 1600)	*Folio*
	MUCH ADO ABOUT NOTHING	1600
	MERRY WIVES OF WINDSOR (*pirated* 1602)	*Folio*
	AS YOU LIKE IT	*Folio*
	JULIUS CAESAR	*Folio*
	TROYLUS AND CRESSIDA	1609
1601–1608	HAMLET (*pirated* 1603)	1604
	TWELFTH NIGHT	*Folio*
	MEASURE FOR MEASURE	*Folio*
	ALL'S WELL THAT ENDS WELL	*Folio*
	OTHELLO	1622
	LEAR	1608
	MACBETH	*Folio*
	TIMON OF ATHENS	*Folio*
	ANTONY AND CLEOPATRA	*Folio*
	CORIOLANUS	*Folio*
After 1608	PERICLES (*omitted from the Folio*)	1609
	CYMBELINE	*Folio*
	THE WINTER'S TALE	*Folio*
	THE TEMPEST	*Folio*
	HENRY VIII	*Folio*

POEMS

DATES UNKNOWN	VENUS AND ADONIS	1593
	THE RAPE OF LUCRECE	1594
	SONNETS A LOVER'S COMPLAINT }	1609
	THE PHOENIX AND THE TURTLE	1601

WILLIAM SHAKESPEARE

William Shakespeare was born at Stratford upon Avon in April, 1564. He was the third child, and eldest son, of John Shakespeare and Mary Arden. His father was one of the most prosperous men of Stratford, who held in turn the chief offices in the town. His mother was of gentle birth, the daughter of Robert Arden of Wilmcote. In December, 1582, Shakespeare married Ann Hathaway, daughter of a farmer of Shottery, near Stratford; their first child Susanna was baptized on May 6, 1583, and twins, Hamnet and Judith, on February 22, 1585. Little is known of Shakespeare's early life; but it is unlikely that a writer who dramatized such an incomparable range and variety of human kinds and experiences should have spent his early manhood entirely in placid pursuits in a country town. There is one tradition, not universally accepted, that he fled from Stratford because he was in trouble for deer stealing, and had fallen foul of Sir Thomas Lucy, the local magnate; another that he was for some time a schoolmaster.

From 1592 onwards the records are much fuller. In March, 1592, the Lord Strange's players produced a new play at the Rose Theatre called *Harry the Sixth*, which was very successful, and was probably the *First Part of Henry VI*. In the autumn of 1592 Robert Greene, the best known of the professional writers, as he was dying wrote a letter to three fellow writers in which he warned them against the ingratitude of players in general, and in particular against an 'upstart crow' who 'supposes he is as much able to bombast out a blank verse as the best of you: and being an absolute Johannes Factotum is in his own conceit the only

Shake-scene in a country.' This is the first reference to Shakespeare, and the whole passage suggests that Shakespeare had become suddenly famous as a playwright. At this time Shakespeare was brought into touch with Edward Alleyne the great tragedian, and Christopher Marlowe, whose thundering parts of Tamburlaine, the Jew of Malta, and Dr Faustus Alleyne was acting, as well as Hieronimo, the hero of Kyd's *Spanish Tragedy*, the most famous of all Elizabethan plays.

In April, 1593, Shakespeare published his poem *Venus and Adonis*, which was dedicated to the young Earl of Southampton: it was a great and lasting success, and was reprinted nine times in the next few years. In May, 1594, his second poem, *The Rape of Lucrece*, was also dedicated to Southampton.

There was little playing in 1593, for the theatres were shut during a severe outbreak of the plague; but in the autumn of 1594, when the plague ceased, the playing companies were reorganized, and Shakespeare became a sharer in the Lord Chamberlain's company who went to play in the Theatre in Shoreditch. During these months Marlowe and Kyd had died. Shakespeare was thus for a time without a rival. He had already written the three parts of *Henry VI*, *Richard III*, *Titus Andronicus*, *The Two Gentlemen of Verona*, *Love's Labour's Lost*, *The Comedy of Errors*, and *The Taming of the Shrew*. Soon afterwards he wrote the first of his greater plays – *Romeo and Juliet* – and he followed this success in the next three years with *A Midsummer Night's Dream*, *Richard II*, and *The Merchant of Venice*. The two parts of *Henry IV*, introducing Falstaff, the most popular of all his comic characters, were written in 1597-8.

The company left the Theatre in 1597 owing to disputes over a renewal of the ground lease, and went to play at the

Curtain in the same neighbourhood. The disputes contin-
ued throughout 1598, and at Christmas the players settled
the matter by demolishing the old Theatre and re-erecting
a new playhouse on the South bank of the Thames, near
Southwark Cathedral. This playhouse was named the
Globe. The expenses of the new building were shared by
the chief members of the Company, including Shakespeare,
who was now a man of some means. In 1596 he had bought
New Place, a large house in the centre of Stratford, for £60,
and through his father purchased a coat-of-arms from the
Heralds, which was the official recognition that he and his
family were gentlefolk.

By the summer of 1598 Shakespeare was recognized as
the greatest of English dramatists. Booksellers were printing his more popular plays, at times even in pirated or stolen
versions, and he received a remarkable tribute from a young
writer named Francis Meres, in his book *Palladis Tamia*. In
a long catalogue of English authors Meres gave Shakespeare
more prominence than any other writer, and mentioned by
name twelve of his plays.

Shortly before the Globe was opened, Shakespeare had
completed the cycle of plays dealing with the whole story
of the Wars of the Roses with *Henry V*. It was followed by
As You Like It, and *Julius Caesar*, the first of the maturer
tragedies. In the next three years he wrote *Troylus and
Cressida*, *The Merry Wives of Windsor*, *Hamlet*, and *Twelfth
Night*.

On March 24, 1603, Queen Elizabeth I died. The company had often performed before her, but they found her
successor a far more enthusiastic patron. One of the first acts
of King James was to take over the company and to pro-
mote them to be his own servants, so that henceforward
they were known as the King's Men. They acted now very

frequently at Court, and prospered accordingly. In the early years of the reign Shakespeare wrote the more sombre comedies, *All's Well that Ends Well*, and *Measure for Measure*, which were followed by *Othello, Macbeth*, and *King Lear*. Then he returned to Roman themes with *Antony and Cleopatra* and *Coriolanus*.

Since 1601 Shakespeare had been writing less, and there were now a number of rival dramatists who were introducing new styles of drama, particularly Ben Jonson (whose first successful comedy, *Every Man in his Humour*, was acted by Shakespeare's company in 1598), Chapman, Dekker, Marston, and Beaumont and Fletcher who began to write in 1607. In 1608 the King's Men acquired a second playhouse, an indoor private theatre in the fashionable quarter of the Blackfriars. At private theatres, plays were performed indoors; the prices charged were higher than in the public playhouses, and the audience consequently was more select. Shakespeare seems to have retired from the stage about this time: his name does not occur in the various lists of players after 1607. Henceforward he lived for the most part at Stratford, where he was regarded as one of the most important citizens. He still wrote a few plays, and he tried his hand at the new form of tragi-comedy – a play with tragic incidents but a happy ending – which Beaumont and Fletcher had popularized. He wrote four of these – *Pericles, Cymbeline, The Winter's Tale*, and *The Tempest*, which was acted at Court in 1611. For the last four years of his life he lived in retirement. His son Hamnet had died in 1596: his two daughters were now married. Shakespeare died at Stratford upon Avon on April 23, 1616, and was buried in the chancel of the church, before the high altar. Shortly afterwards a memorial which still exists, with a portrait bust, was set up on the North wall. His wife survived him.

When Shakespeare died fourteen of his plays had been separately published in Quarto booklets. In 1623 his surviving fellow actors, John Heming and Henry Condell, with the co-operation of a number of printers, published a collected edition of thirty-six plays in one Folio volume, with an engraved portrait, memorial verses by Ben Jonson and others, and an Epistle to the Reader in which Heming and Condell make the interesting note that Shakespeare's 'hand and mind went together, and what he thought, he uttered with that easiness that we have scarce received from him a blot in his papers'.

The plays as printed in the Quartos or the Folio differ considerably from the usual modern text. They are often not divided into scenes, and sometimes not even into acts. Nor are there place-headings at the beginning of each scene, because in the Elizabethan theatre there was no scenery. They are carelessly printed and the spelling is erratic.

THE ELIZABETHAN THEATRE

Although plays of one sort and another had been acted for many generations, no permanent playhouse was erected in England until 1576. In the 1570s the Lord Mayor and Aldermen of the City of London and the players were constantly at variance. As a result James Burbage, then the leader of the great Earl of Leicester's players, decided that he would erect a playhouse outside the jurisdiction of the Lord Mayor, where the players would no longer be hindered by the authorities. Accordingly in 1576 he built the Theatre in Shoreditch, at that time a suburb of London. The experiment was successful, and by 1592 there were two more playhouses in London, the Curtain (also in Shore-ditch), and the Rose on the south bank of the river, near Southwark Cathedral.

Elizabethan players were accustomed to act on a variety of stages; in the great hall of a nobleman's house, or one of the Queen's palaces, in town halls and in yards, as well as their own theatre.

The public playhouse for which most of Shakespeare's plays were written was a small and intimate affair. The outside measurement of the Fortune Theatre, which was built in 1600 to rival the new Globe, was but eighty feet square. Playhouses were usually circular or octagonal, with three tiers of galleries looking down upon the yard or pit, which was open to the sky. The stage jutted out into the yard so that the actors came forward into the midst of their audience.

Over the stage there was a roof, and on either side doors by which the characters entered or disappeared. Over the back of the stage ran a gallery or upper stage, with windows on either side, which was used whenever an upper scene was needed, as when Romeo climbs up to Juliet's bedroom, or the citizens of Angiers address King John from the walls. The space beneath this upper stage was known as the tiring house; it was concealed from the audience by a curtain which would be drawn back to reveal an inner stage, for such scenes as the witches' cave in *Macbeth*, Prospero's cell, or Juliet's tomb.

There was no general curtain concealing the whole stage, so that all scenes on the main stage began with an entrance and ended with an exit. Thus in tragedies the dead must be carried away. There was no scenery, and therefore no limit to the number of scenes, for a scene came to an end when the characters left the stage. When it was necessary for the

THE GLOBE THEATRE

Wood-engraving by R. J. Beedham after a reconstruction by J. C. Adams

exact locality of a scene to be known, then Shakespeare indicated it in the dialogue; otherwise a simple property or a garment was sufficient; a chair or stool showed an indoor scene, a man wearing riding boots was a messenger, a king wearing armour was on the battlefield, or the like. Such simplicity was on the whole an advantage; the spectator was not distracted by the setting and Shakespeare was able to use as many scenes as he wished. The action passed by very quickly: a play of 2500 lines of verse could be acted in two hours. Moreover, since the actor was so close to his audience, the slightest subtlety of voice and gesture was easily appreciated.

The company was a 'Fellowship of Players', who were all partners and sharers. There were usually ten to fifteen full members, with three or four boys, and some paid servants. Shakespeare had therefore to write for his team. The chief actor in the company was Richard Burbage, who first distinguished himself as Richard III; for him Shakespeare wrote his great tragic parts. An important member of the company was the clown or low comedian. From 1594 to 1600 the company's clown was Will Kemp; he was succeeded by Robert Armin. No women were allowed to appear on the stage, and all women's parts were taken by boys.

THE TRAGEDY OF OTHELLO
THE MOOR OF VENICE

There is a record showing that the King's Players were paid
for acting a play called *The Moor of Venice* before the Court
of King James I on the 1st November, 1604. This is the
earliest reference to *The Tragedy of Othello the Moor of Venice*,
which was then probably not more than two years old.

The direct source of the play is not known, but it derived
from a story in the *Hecatomithi* of Giraldi Cinthio, published in Venice in 1566. There lived in Venice a Moor,
who was valiant and handsome, and highly esteemed by
the Signoria of the Republic for his skill in war. A lady
named Desdemona, attracted by his valour, fell in love
with him, and he with her, so that in spite of the objections
of her parents, she married him. They lived in great harmony in Venice. After a time the Signoria appointed the
Moor to command the soldiers to be sent to Cyprus.
Thither the Moor sailed with Desdemona, and after a
peaceful passage, reached the island. Amongst the soldiers
there was an ensign, in high favour with the Moor, who
did not realize that beneath a proud and valorous outside
there lurked a most depraved nature. He also had taken
with him his wife to Cyprus, a young, fair, and virtuous
lady, who soon became friendly with Desdemona. In the
same company there was a certain captain, likewise a
favourite of the Moor. The wicked ensign fell desperately
in love with Desdemona, and sought to reveal his passion,
but as she showed no interest in him, he supposed that she
was in love with the captain. He began to hate both her
and the captain, and to scheme their downfall.

Not long afterwards it happened that the captain, having drawn his sword upon a soldier of the Guard, was deprived of his rank by the Moor. Desdemona was greatly grieved, and endeavoured to reconcile her husband to him. The Moor told the ensign how his wife was importuning him to receive the captain back into favour. Perhaps, the ensign hinted, the Lady Desdemona might have good reason to look kindly on him; and with that he began to throw out hints, which greatly moved the Moor. The Moor, burning with indignation and anguish, demanded proof, which the ensign at first found difficult to obtain; but he noticed that when Desdemona came to visit his wife she carried with her a handkerchief, which her husband had given her, finely embroidered in Moorish fashion. The ensign had a little daughter, much loved by Desdemona. As Desdemona was embracing the child, he drew the handkerchief from her sash so cunningly that she did not notice. He then took the handkerchief and left it on the captain's bed.

By this means the ensign was able to persuade the Moor that his wife had given the handkerchief to her lover. The captain had a wife who was expert at embroidery work, and she began to copy the work on the handkerchief; while she was so engaged, the ensign observed her and pointed her out to the Moor, who was thereby entirely convinced of his wife's guilt. The Moor now prayed the ensign to kill the captain. At first he was unwilling, but at length, being richly paid, he agreed. One night he met the captain on his way to visit a courtesan, and struck him such a blow on the right thigh that he cut off his leg and felled him to the ground. Next morning news of the affair reached Desdemona, who showed the greatest grief. This served to confirm the Moor's suspicions. He sought out the ensign and they plotted how best to kill Desdemona. At length the ensign suggested that he should beat her with a stocking filled with sand, and when she was dead, pull down part of the ceiling on her to make it appear that she had been killed accidentally. This plan soon after they carried out. On the next morning Desdemona was buried, to the great grief of the people.

Soon the Moor began to feel such sorrow at her loss that he went about as one bereft of reason. Reflecting that the ensign was the cause of his loss he grew to hate him so bitterly that he could not bear to look at him. He would have slain him, had he dared, but instead he deprived him of his rank, and turned him out of his company.

The ensign therefore began to plot against the Moor, and, seeking out the captain, who was by this time recovered, he told him that it was the Moor who had cut off his leg, because of his suspicions, and also that he had slain Desdemona. When he heard this the captain accused the Moor to the Signoria. The ensign corroborated the charge. The Signoria of Venice, when they heard of the cruelty inflicted by a barbarian upon a lady of their city, commanded that the Moor should be brought to Venice, where they sought to draw the truth from him with torture; but he resisted the torture with great firmness and denied everything. After some days in prison he was condemned to perpetual banishment. Ultimately he was killed by the kinsfolk of Desdemona. The ensign also came to a miserable death.

No English version of this tale is known, and it differs in so many details from the play that it is not likely that Shakespeare used it at first hand.

The text of *Othello* is difficult. There are three early versions: a quarto of 1622, the text of the First Folio of 1623 and a later quarto of 1630. All three texts have considerable minor differences. The Folio is the best text, and has obviously been carefully prepared for the printer. The original copy, used by the printer of the Folio, seems to have been made by a professional scribe. It divides the play into Acts and Scenes, and appends a list of Characters, but it omits a few stage directions. It prints about 160 lines which are not to be found in the First Quarto. These may have been cut during performance. On the other hand it omits all the oaths, and has been scrupulously, even morbidly, refined. Even such harmless remarks as 'faith' and 'pray' have been altered or cut out. These are kept in the Quarto. The Quarto text is on the whole inferior to the Folio. It adds a few lines omitted by the Folio, but where there are differences of reading the Quarto is usually weaker. It seems probable that the Quarto was printed from an earlier copy of the playhouse manuscript, and the Folio from a later copy, revised and bowdlerized. The text of the play to be found in modern editions is compounded of the First Quarto and the Folio, with preference given usually to the Folio. The present text follows the Folio more closely. The oaths have been put back, spelling has been modernized but the original arrangement and the punctuation have been kept except in a few places where they seemed indefensible. Elizabethan punctuation was used to 'point' the text for reading aloud, and in places the Folio punctuation of *Othello* is very subtle. A typical example of the differences between the various versions is to be found in Othello's great speech before he murders Desdemona. The First Quarto reads:

> when I haue pluckt the rose,
> I cannot giue it vitall growth againe,
> It must needes wither; I'le smell it on the tree,

A balmy breath, that doth almost perswade
Iustice her selfe to breake her sword once more,
Be thus, when thou art dead, and I will kill thee,
And loue thee after: once more, and this the last,
So sweet was ne're so fatall.

The 'accepted' text prints this speech as follows:

When I have pluck'd the rose,
I cannot give it vital growth again,
It needs must wither: I'll smell it on the tree.
O balmy breath, that dost almost persuade
Justice to break her sword! One more, one more.
Be thus when thou art dead, and I will kill thee,
And love thee after. One more, and this the last:
So sweet was ne'er so fatal.

The Folio text will be found on page 125.

   The reader who is used to the 'accepted' text may thus find certain unfamiliarities, but the present text is nearer to that used in Shakespeare's own playhouse.

The Tragedy of Othello
the Moor of Venice

THE ACTORS' NAMES

OTHELLO, the Moor
BRABANTIO, Father to Desdemona
CASSIO, an Honourable Lieutenant
IAGO, a villain
RODERIGO, a gull'd Gentleman
DUKE OF VENICE
SENATORS
MONTANO, Governor of Cyprus
GENTLEMEN OF CYPRUS
LODOVICO, and GRATIANO, two Noble Venetians
Sailors
Clown

DESDEMONA, wife to Othello
EMILIA, wife to Iago
BIANCA, a Courtesan

I.1

Enter Roderigo, and Iago.

RODERIGO: Never tell me, I take it much unkindly
That thou (Iago) who hast had my purse,
As if the strings were thine, shouldst know of this.   5
IAGO: 'Sblood, but you 'll not hear me. If ever I did dream
Of such a matter, abhor me.
RODERIGO: Thou told'st me,
Thou didst hold him in thy hate.   10
IAGO: Despise me
If I do not. Three Great-ones of the City
(In personal suit to make me his Lieutenant)
Off-capp'd to him: and by the faith of man
I know my price, I am worth no worse a place.   15
But he (as loving his own pride, and purposes)
Evades them, with a bumbast circumstance,
Horribly stuff'd with epithets of war,
And in conclusion,
Nonsuits my mediators. For certes, says he,   20
I have already chose my officer. And what was he?
Forsooth, a great arithmetician,
One Michael Cassio, a Florentine,
(A fellow almost damn'd in a fair wife)
That never set a squadron in the field,   25
Nor the division of a battle knows
More than a spinster. Unless the bookish theoric:
Wherein the toged Consuls can propose
As masterly as he. Mere prattle (without practice)
Is all his soldiership. But he (Sir) had th' election;   30

And I (of whom his eyes had seen the proof
At Rhodes, at Cyprus, and on other grounds,
Christen'd, and Heathen,) must be be-leed, and calm'd
By debitor, and creditor. This counter-caster,
5   He (in good time) must his Lieutenant be,
And I (God bless the mark) his Moorship's Ancient.

RODERIGO: By heaven, I rather would have been his hangman.

IAGO: Why, there's no remedy.
10   'Tis the curse of service;
Preferment goes by letter, and affection,
Not by old gradation, where each second
Stood heir to th' first. Now Sir, be judge yourself,
Whether I in any just term am affin'd
15   To love the Moor?

RODERIGO: I would not follow him then.

IAGO: O Sir content you.
I follow him, to serve my turn upon him.
We cannot all be masters, nor all masters
20   Cannot be truly follow'd. You shall mark
Many a duteous and knee-crooking knave;
That (doting on his own obsequious bondage)
Wears out his time, much like his master's ass,
For nought but provender, and when he 's old cashier'd.
25   Whip me such honest knaves. Others there are
Who trimm'd in forms, and visages of duty,
Keep yet their hearts attending on themselves,
And throwing but shows of service on their Lords
Do well thrive by them.
30   And when they have lin'd their coats
Do themselves homage.
These fellows have some soul,
And such a one do I profess myself. For (Sir)

It is as sure as you are Roderigo,
Were I the Moor, I would not be Iago:
In following him, I follow but myself.
Heaven is my judge, not I for love and duty,
But seeming so, for my peculiar end: 5
For when my outward action doth demonstrate
The native act, and figure of my heart
In complement extern, 'tis not long after
But I will wear my heart upon my sleeve
For daws to peck at; I am not what I am.   10

RODERIGO: What a full fortune does the thick-lips owe
  If he can carry 't thus?

IAGO: Call up her father:
  Rouse him, make after him, poison his delight,
  Proclaim him in the streets. Incense her kinsmen,   15
  And though he in a fertile climate dwell,
  Plague him with flies: though that his joy be joy,
  Yet throw such chances of vexation on 't,
  As it may lose some colour.

RODERIGO: Here is her father's house, I 'll call aloud.   20

IAGO: Do, with like timorous accent, and dire yell,
  As when (by night and negligence) the fire
  Is spied in populous cities.

RODERIGO: What hoa: Brabantio, Signior Brabantio,
  hoa.   25

IAGO: Awake: what hoa, Brabantio: thieves, thieves.
  Look to your house, your daughter, and your bags,
  Thieves, thieves.

Enter Brabantio at a window.

BRABANTIO: What is the reason of this terrible sum-   30
  mons? What is the matter there?

RODERIGO: Signior is all your family within?

IAGO: Are your doors lock'd?

BRABANTIO: Why? Wherefore ask you this?

IAGO: Sir, y'are robb'd, for shame put on your gown,
Your heart is burst, you have lost half your soul;
Even now, now, very now, an old black ram
5 Is tupping your white ewe. Arise, arise,
Awake the snorting citizens with the bell,
Or else the devil will make a grandsire of you.
Arise I say.

BRABANTIO: What, have you lost your wits?

10 RODERIGO: Most reverend Signior, do you know my
voice?

BRABANTIO: Not I: what are you?

RODERIGO: My name is Roderigo.

BRABANTIO: The worser welcome:
15 I have charg'd thee not to haunt about my doors:
In honest plainness thou hast heard me say,
My daughter is not for thee. And now in madness
(Being full of supper, and distemp'ring draughts)
Upon malicious knavery, dost thou come
20 To start my quiet.

RODERIGO: Sir, Sir, Sir.

BRABANTIO: But thou must needs be sure,
My spirits and my place have in their power
To make this bitter to thee.

25 RODERIGO: Patience good Sir.

BRABANTIO: What tell'st thou me of robbing?
This is Venice: my house is not a grange.

RODERIGO: Most grave Brabantio,
In simple and pure soul, I come to you.

30 IAGO: Sir: you are one of those that will not serve God,
if the devil bid you. Because we come to do you service,
and you think we are ruffians, you 'll have your daughter
cover'd with a Barbary horse, you 'll have your nephews

neigh to you, you 'll have coursers for cousins: and
gennets for germans. Ponies for family relations.

BRABANTIO: What profane wretch art thou?

IAGO: I am one, Sir, that come to tell you, your daughter
and the Moor, are making the beast with two backs.   5

BRABANTIO: Thou art a villain.

IAGO: You are a Senator.

BRABANTIO: This thou shalt answer. I know thee
Roderigo.

RODERIGO: Sir, I will answer any thing. But I beseech you   10
If 't be your pleasure, and most wise consent,
(As partly I find it is) that your fair daughter,
At this odd even and dull watch o' th' night
Transported with no worse nor better guard,
But with a knave of common hire, a gondolier,   15
To the gross clasps of a lascivious Moor:
If this be known to you, and your allowance,
We then have done you bold, and saucy wrongs.
But if you know not this, my manners tell me,
We have your wrong rebuke. Do not believe   20
That from the sense of all civility,
I thus would play and trifle with your reverence.
Your daughter (if you have not given her leave)
I say again, hath made a gross revolt,
Tying her duty, beauty, wit, and fortunes   25
In an extravagant, and wheeling stranger,
Of here, and every where: straight satisfy yourself.
If she be in her chamber, or your house,
Let loose on me the justice of the State
For thus deluding you.   30

BRABANTIO: Strike on the tinder, hoa:
Give me a taper: call up all my people,
This accident is not unlike my dream,

Belief of it oppresses me already.
Light, I say, light.   *Exit.*

IAGO: Farewell: for I must leave you.
It seems not meet, nor wholesome to my place
5   To be producted (as if I stay, I shall)
Against the Moor. For I do know the State,
(However this may gall him with some check)
Cannot with safety cast him. For he 's embark'd
With such loud reason to the Cyprus Wars,
10   (Which even now stands in act) that for their souls
Another of his fadom, they have none,
To lead their business. In which regard,
Though I do hate him as I do hell pains,
Yet, for necessity of present life,
15   I must show out a flag, and sign of love,
(Which is indeed but sign) that you shall surely find him:
Lead to the Sagittary, the raised search:
And there will I be with him. So farewell.
                    Exit.
20   *Enter Brabantio, in his night-gown, and Servants*
                with torches.

BRABANTIO: It is too true an evil. Gone she is,
And what 's to come of my despised time,
Is nought but bitterness. Now Roderigo,
25   Where didst thou see her? (Oh unhappy girl)
With the Moor say'st thou? (Who would be a father?)
How didst thou know 'twas she? (Oh she deceives me
Past thought): what said she to you? Get moe tapers:
Raise all my kindred. Are they married think you?
30 RODERIGO: Truly I think they are.
BRABANTIO: Oh Heaven: how got she out?
Oh treason of the blood.
Fathers, from hence trust not your daughters' minds

By what you see them act. Is there not charms,
By which the property of youth, and maidhood
May be abus'd? Have you not read Roderigo,
Of some such thing?

RODERIGO: Yes sir: I have indeed.   5

BRABANTIO: Call up my brother: oh would you had had
   her.
   Some one way, some another. Do you know
   Where we may apprehend her, and the Moor?

RODERIGO: I think I can discover him, if you please   10
   To get good guard, and go along with me.

BRABANTIO: Pray you lead on. At every house I'll call,
   (I may command at most): get weapons (hoa)
   And raise some special officers of might:
   On good Roderigo, I will deserve your pains.   15
                        Exeunt.

I.2

Enter Othello, Iago, Attendants, with torches.

IAGO: Though in the trade of war I have slain men,
   Yet do I hold it very stuff o' th' conscience   20
   To do no contriv'd murder: I lack iniquity
   Sometime to do me service. Nine, or ten times
   I had thought t' have yerk'd him here under the ribs.

OTHELLO: 'Tis better as it is.

IAGO: Nay but he prated,   25
   And spoke such scurvy, and provoking terms
   Against your Honour, that with the little godliness I
      have
   I did full hard forbear him. But I pray you Sir,
   Are you fast married? Be assur'd of this,   30
   That the Magnifico is much belov'd,

And hath in his effect a voice potential
As double as the Duke's: He will divorce you,
Or put upon you, what restraint or grievance,
The Law (with all his might, to enforce it on)
5   Will give him cable.

OTHELLO: Let him do his spite;
My services, which I have done the Signiory
Shall out-tongue his complaints. 'Tis yet to know,
Which when I know, that boasting is an honour,
10   I shall promulgate. I fetch my life and being,
From men of royal siege. And my demerits
May speak (unbonneted) to as proud a fortune
As this that I have reach'd. For know Iago,
But that I love the gentle Desdemona,
15   I would not my unhoused free condition
Put into circumscription, and confine,
For the sea's worth. But look, what lights come yond?
                  Enter Cassio, with torches.

IAGO: Those are the raised father, and his friends:
20   You were best go in.

OTHELLO: Not I: I must be found.
My parts, my title, and my perfect soul
Shall manifest me rightly. Is it they?

IAGO: By Janus, I think no.

25 OTHELLO: The servants of the Duke's?
And my Lieutenant?
The goodness of the night upon you (friends)
What is the news?

CASSIO: The Duke does greet you (General)
30   And he requires your haste, post-haste appearance,
Even on the instant.

OTHELLO: What is the matter, think you?

CASSIO: Something from Cyprus, as I may divine:

It is a business of some heat. The galleys
Have sent a dozen sequent messengers
This very night, at one another's heels:
And many of the Consuls, rais'd and met,
Are at the Duke's already. You have been hotly call'd   5
    for,
When being not at your lodging to be found,
The Senate hath sent about three several quests,
To search you out.

OTHELLO: 'Tis well I am found by you: 10
I will but spend a word here in the house,
And go with you.

CASSIO: Ancient, what makes he here?

IAGO: Faith, he tonight hath boarded a land carrack,
If it prove lawful prize, he's made for ever.   15

CASSIO: I do not understand.

IAGO: He's married.

CASSIO: To who?

IAGO: Marry to – Come Captain, will you go?

OTHELLO: Have with you.   20

CASSIO: Here comes another troop to seek for you.
    Enter Brabantio, Roderigo, with officers, and torches.

IAGO: It is Brabantio: General be advis'd,
He comes to bad intent.

OTHELLO: Holla, stand there.   25

RODERIGO: Signior, it is the Moor.

BRABANTIO: Down with him, thief.

IAGO: You, Roderigo? Come sir, I am for you.

OTHELLO: Keep up your bright swords, for the dew will
    rust them.   30
Good Signior, you shall more command with years,
Than with your weapons.

BRABANTIO: Oh thou foul thief,

Where hast thou stow'd my daughter?
Damn'd as thou art, thou hast enchanted her
For I 'll refer me to all things of sense,
(If she in chains of magic were not bound)
5   Whether a maid, so tender, fair, and happy,
So opposite to marriage, that she shunn'd
The wealthy curled darling of our Nation,
Would ever have (t' incur a general mock)
Run from her guardage to the sooty bosom,
10   Of such a thing as thou: to fear, not to delight?
Judge me the world, if 'tis not gross in sense,
That thou hast practis'd on her with foul charms,
Abus'd her delicate youth, with drugs or minerals,
That weakens motion. I 'll have 't disputed on,
15   'Tis probable, and palpable to thinking;
I therefore apprehend and do attach thee,
For an abuser of the World, a practiser
Of arts inhibited, and out of warrant;
Lay hold upon him, if he do resist
20   Subdue him, at his peril.
  OTHELLO: Hold your hands
Both you of my inclining, and the rest.
Were it my cue to fight, I should have known it
Without a prompter. Whither will you that I go
25   To answer this your charge?
  BRABANTIO: To prison, till fit time
Of Law, and course of direct Session
Call thee to answer.
  OTHELLO: What if I do obey?
30   How may the Duke be therewith satisfi'd,
Whose messengers are here about my side,
Upon some present business of the State,
To bring me to him.

OFFICER: 'Tis true most worthy Signior,
  The Duke 's in Council, and your noble self,
  I am sure is sent for.

BRABANTIO: How? The Duke in Council?
  In this time of the night? Bring him away: 5
  Mine's not an idle cause. The Duke himself,
  Or any of my brothers of the State,
  Cannot but feel this wrong, as 'twere their own:
  For if such actions may have passage free,
  Bond-slaves, and pagans shall our Statesmen be.   10

Exeunt.

I. 3

*The Duke and Senators set at a table with lights
and Attendants.*

DUKE: There is no composition in this news,   15
  That gives them credit.

1 SENATOR: Indeed, they are disproportioned;
  My letters say, a hundred and seven galleys.

DUKE: And mine a hundred and forty.

2 SENATOR: And mine two hundred: 20
  But though they jump not on a just accompt,
  (As in these cases where the aim reports,
  'Tis oft with difference) yet do they all confirm
  A Turkish fleet, and bearing up to Cyprus.

DUKE: Nay, it is possible enough to judgement: 25
  I do not so secure me in the error,
  But the main article I do approve
  In fearful sense.

SAILOR *within:* What hoa, what hoa, what hoa.

Enter Sailor.   30

OFFICER: A messenger from the galleys.

DUKE: Now? What's the business?

SAILOR: The Turkish preparation makes for Rhodes,
    So was I bid report here to the State,
    By Signior Angelo.

5 DUKE: How say you by this change?

1 SENATOR: This cannot be
    By no assay of reason. 'Tis a pageant
    To keep us in false gaze, when we consider
    Th' importancy of Cyprus to the Turk;
10   And let ourselves again but understand,
    That as it more concerns the Turk than Rhodes, ·
    So may he with more facile question bear it,
    For that it stands not in such warlike brace,
    But altogether lacks th' abilities
15   That Rhodes is dress'd in. If we make thought of this,
    We must not think the Turk is so unskilful,
    To leave that latest, which concerns him first,
    Neglecting an attempt of ease, and gain
    To wake, and wage a danger profitless.

20 DUKE: Nay, in all confidence he's not for Rhodes.

OFFICER: Here is more news.

Enter a Messenger.

MESSENGER: The Ottomites, reverend, and gracious,
    Steering with due course toward the Isle of Rhodes,
25   Have there injointed them with an after fleet.

1 SENATOR: Ay, so I thought: how many, as you guess?

MESSENGER: Of thirty sail: and now they do re-stem
    Their backward course, bearing with frank appearance
    Their purposes towards Cyprus. Signior Montano,
30   Your trusty and most valiant servitor,
    With his free duty, recommends you thus,
    And prays you to believe him.

DUKE: 'Tis certain then for Cyprus:

Marcus Luccicos is not he in town?

1 SENATOR: He's now in Florence.

DUKE: Write from us,
To him post, post-haste, dispatch.

1 SENATOR: Here comes Brabantio, and the valiant Moor. 5
Enter Brabantio, Othello, Cassio, Iago, Roderigo,
and Officers.

DUKE: Valiant Othello, we must straight employ you,
Against the general enemy Ottoman.
I did not see you: welcome gentle Signior, 10
We lack'd your counsel, and your help tonight.

BRABANTIO: So did I yours: Good your Grace pardon me.
Neither my place, nor aught I heard of business
Hath rais'd me from my bed; nor doth the general care
Take hold on me. For my particular grief 15
Is of so flood-gate, and o'erbearing nature,
That it engluts, and swallows other sorrows,
And it is still itself.

DUKE: Why? What's the matter?

BRABANTIO: My daughter: oh my daughter! 20

SENATORS: Dead?

BRABANTIO: Ay, to me.
She is abus'd, stol'n from me, and corrupted
By spells, and medicines, bought of mountebanks;
For Nature, so prepost'rously to err, 25
(Being not deficient, blind, or lame of sense,)
Sans witchcraft could not.

DUKE: Whoe'er he be, that in this foul proceeding
Hath thus beguil'd your daughter of herself,
And you of her; the bloody Book of Law, 30
You shall yourself read, in the bitter letter,
After your own sense: yea, though our proper son
Stood in your action.

BRABANTIO: Humbly I thank your Grace,
Here is the man; this Moor, whom now it seems
Your special mandate, for the state affairs
Hath hither brought.

5 ALL: We are very sorry for 't.

DUKE: What in your own part, can you say to this?

BRABANTIO: Nothing, but this is so.

OTHELLO: Most potent, grave, and reverend Signiors,
My very noble, and approv'd good masters;
10   That I have ta'en away this old man's daughter,
It is most true: true I have married her;
The very head, and front of my offending,
Hath this extent; no more. Rude am I, in my speech,
And little blest with the soft phrase of peace;
15   For since these arms of mine, had seven years' pith,
Till now, some nine moons wasted, they have us'd
Their dearest action, in the tented field:
And little of this great world can I speak,
More than pertains to feats of broils, and battle,
20   And therefore little shall I grace my cause,
In speaking for myself. Yet, (by your gracious patience)
I will a round unvarnish'd tale deliver,
Of my whole course of love.
What drugs, what charms,
25   What conjuration, and what mighty magic,
(For such proceeding am I charg'd withal)
I won his daughter.

BRABANTIO: A maiden, never bold:
Of spirit so still, and quiet, that her motion
30   Blush'd at herself, and she, in spite of nature,
Of years, of country, credit, every thing,
To fall in love, with what she fear'd to look on;
It is a judgement maim'd, and most imperfect,

That will confess Perfection so could err
Against all rules of Nature, and must be driven
To find out practices of cunning hell
Why this should be. I therefore vouch again,
That with some mixtures, powerful o'er the blood,   5
Or with some dram, (conjur'd to this effect),
He wrought upon her.

DUKE: To vouch this, is no proof,
Without more wider, and more overt test
Than these thin habits, and poor likelihoods   10
Of modern seeming, do prefer against him.

SENATOR: But Othello, speak,
Did you, by indirect, and forced courses
Subdue, and poison this young maid's affections?
Or came it by request, and such fair question   15
As soul to soul affordeth?

OTHELLO: I do beseech you,
Send for the Lady to the Sagittary,
And let her speak of me before her father:
If you do find me foul, in her report,   20
The trust, the office, I do hold of you,
Not only take away, but let your sentence
Even fall upon my life.

DUKE: Fetch Desdemona hither.

Exit two or three.   25

OTHELLO: Ancient, conduct them:
You best know the place.

Exit Iago.

And till she come, as truly as to heaven,
I do confess the vices of my blood,   30
So justly to your grave ears, I 'll present,
How I did thrive in this fair Lady's love,
And she in mine.

DUKE: Say it Othello.

OTHELLO: Her father lov'd me, oft invited me:
Still question'd me the story of my life,
From year to year: the battles, sieges, fortune,
5   That I have pass'd.
I ran it through, even from my boyish days,
To th' very moment that he bad me tell it.
Wherein I spoke of most disastrous chances:
Of moving accidents by flood and field,
10   Of hair-breadth 'scapes i' th' imminent deadly breach;
Of being taken by the insolent foe,
And sold to slavery. Of my redemption thence,
And portance in my traveller's history.
Wherein of antres vast, and deserts idle,
15   Rough quarries, rocks, hills, whose heads touch heaven,
It was my hint to speak. Such was my process,
And of the Cannibals that each other eat,
The Anthropophagi, and men whose heads
Do grow beneath their shoulders. These things to hear,
20   Would Desdemona seriously incline:
But still the house affairs would draw her hence:
Which ever as she could with haste dispatch,
She 'ld come again, and with a greedy ear
Devour up my discourse. Which I observing,
25   Took once a pliant hour, and found good means
To draw from her a prayer of earnest heart,
That I would all my pilgrimage dilate,
Whereof by parcels she had something heard,
But not intentively: I did consent,
30   And often did beguile her of her tears,
When I did speak of some distressful stroke
That my youth suffer'd: My story being done,
She gave me for my pains a world of sighs;

She swore in faith 'twas strange: 'twas passing strange,
'Twas pitiful: 'twas wondrous pitiful.
She wish'd she had not heard it, yet she wish'd
That Heaven had made her such a man. She thank'd me,
And bad me, if I had a friend that lov'd her,   5
I should but teach him how to tell my story,
And that would woo her. Upon this hint I spake,
She lov'd me for the dangers I had pass'd,
And I lov'd her, that she did pity them.
This only is the witchcraft I have us'd.   10
Here comes the Lady: Let her witness it.
          Enter Desdemona, Iago, Attendants.
DUKE: I think this tale would win my daughter too,
     Good Brabantio, take up this mangled matter at the
        best: 15
     Men do their broken weapons rather use,
     Than their bare hands.
BRABANTIO: I pray you hear her speak.
     If she confess that she was half the wooer,
     Destruction on my head, if my bad blame   20
     Light on the man. Come hither gentle Mistress,
     Do you perceive in all this noble company,
     Where most you owe obedience?
DESDEMONA: My noble father,
     I do perceive here a divided duty.   25
     To you I am bound for life, and education:
     My life and education both do learn me,
     How to respect you. You are the Lord of duty,
     I am hitherto your daughter. But here 's my husband;
     And so much duty, as my mother show'd   30
     To you, preferring you before her father:
     So much I challenge, that I may profess
     Due to the Moor my Lord.

BRABANTIO: God be with you: I have done.
Please it your Grace, on to the state affairs;
I had rather to adopt a child, than get it.
Come hither Moor;
5   I here do give thee that with all my heart,
Which but thou hast already, with all my heart
I would keep from thee. For your sake (Jewel)
I am glad at soul, I have no other child,
For thy escape would teach me tyranny
10   To hang clogs on them. I have done my Lord.
DUKE: Let me speak like yourself:
And lay a sentence,
Which as a grise, or step may help these lovers.
When remedies are past, the griefs are ended
15   By seeing the worst, which late on hopes depended.
To mourn a mischief that is past and gone,
Is the next way to draw new mischief on.
What cannot be preserv'd, when Fortune takes:
Patience, her injury a mock'ry makes.
20   The robb'd that smiles, steals something from the thief,
He robs himself, that spends a bootless grief.
BRABANTIO: So let the Turk of Cyprus us beguile,
We lose it not so long as we can smile:
He bears the sentence well, that nothing bears,
25   But the free comfort which from thence he hears.
But he bears both the sentence, and the sorrow,
That to pay grief, must of poor Patience borrow.
These sentences, to sugar, or to gall,
Being strong on both sides, are equivocal.
30   But words are words, I never yet did hear
That the bruis'd heart was pierc'd through the ear.
I humbly beseech you proceed to th' affairs of State.
DUKE: The Turk with a most mighty preparation makes

for Cyprus: Othello, the fortitude of the place is best
known to you. And though we have there a substitute of
most allowed sufficiency; yet opinion, a more sovereign
mistress of effects, throws a more safer voice on you:
you must therefore be content to slubber the gloss of   5
your new fortunes, with this more stubborn, and
boist'rous expedition.

OTHELLO: The Tyrant Custom, most grave Senators,
Hath made the flinty and steel couch of War
My thrice-driven bed of down. I do agnize   10
A natural and prompt alacrity,
I find in hardness: and do undertake
This present wars against the Ottomites.
Most humbly therefore bending to your State,
I crave fit disposition for my wife,   15
Due reference of place, and exhibition,
With such accommodation and besort
As levels with her breeding.

DUKE: Why, at her father's.

BRABANTIO: I will not have it so.   20

OTHELLO: Nor I.

DESDEMONA: Nor would I there reside,
To put my father in impatient thoughts
By being in his eye. Most gracious Duke,
To my unfolding, lend your prosperous ear,   25
And let me find a charter in your voice
T' assist my simpleness.

DUKE: What would you Desdemona?

DESDEMONA: That I did love the Moor, to live with him,
My downright violence, and storm of fortunes,   30
May trumpet to the world. My heart's subdu'd
Even to the very quality of my Lord;
I saw Othello's visage in his mind,

And to his honours and his valiant parts,
Did I my soul and fortunes consecrate.
So that (dear Lords) if I be left behind
A moth of peace, and he go to the war,
5   The rites for why I love him, are bereft me:
And I a heavy interim shall support
By his dear absence. Let me go with him.
OTHELLO: Let her have your voice.
Vouch with me Heaven, I therefore beg it not
10   To please the palate of my appetite:
Nor to comply with heat the young affects
In my defunct, and proper satisfaction.
But to be free, and bounteous to her mind:
And Heaven defend your good souls, that you think
15   I will your serious and great business scant
When she is with me. No, when light-wing'd toys
Of feather'd Cupid, seel with wanton dullness
My speculative, and offic'd instrument:
That my disports corrupt, and taint my business:
20   Let housewives make a skillet of my helm,
And all indign, and base adversities,
Make head against my estimation.
DUKE: Be it as you shall privately determine,
Either for her stay, or going: th' affair cries haste:
25   And speed must answer it.
SENATOR: You must away tonight.
OTHELLO: With all my heart.
DUKE: At nine i' th' morning, here we 'll meet again.
Othello, leave some officer behind
30   And he shall our commission bring to you:
And such things else of quality and respect
As doth import you.
OTHELLO: So please your Grace, my Ancient,

A man he is of honesty and trust:
To his conveyance I assign my wife,
With what else needful, your good Grace shall think
To be sent after me.

DUKE: Let it be so: 5
Good night to every one. And noble Signior,
If virtue no delighted beauty lack,
Your son-in-law is far more fair than black.

SENATOR: Adieu brave Moor, use Desdemona well.

BRABANTIO: Look to her (Moor) if thou hast eyes to see: 10
She has deceiv'd her father, and may thee.
Exeunt Duke, Senators, Officers, &c.

OTHELLO: My life upon her faith. Honest Iago,
My Desdemona must I leave to thee:
I prithee let thy wife attend on her,   15
And bring them after in the best advantage.
Come Desdemona, I have but an hour
Of love, of wordly matter, and direction
To spend with thee. We must obey the time.
Exeunt Othello and Desdemona.   20

RODERIGO: Iago.

IAGO: What say'st thou noble heart?

RODERIGO: What will I do, think'st thou?

IAGO: Why go to bed and sleep.

RODERIGO: I will incontinently drown myself.   25

IAGO: If thou dost, I shall never love thee after. Why thou
silly gentleman?

RODERIGO: It is silliness to live, when to live is torment:
and then have we a prescription to die, when death is
our physician.   30

IAGO: Oh villainous: I have look'd upon the world for
four times seven years, and since I could distinguish
betwixt a benefit, and an injury: I never found man

that knew how to love himself. Ere I would say, I would drown myself for the love of a guinea hen, I would change my humanity with a baboon.

RODERIGO: What should I do? I confess it is my shame
5 to be so fond, but it is not in my virtue to amend it.

IAGO: Virtue? A fig, 'tis in ourselves that we are thus, .or thus. Our bodies are our gardens, to the which, our wills are gardeners. So that if we will plant nettles, or sow lettuce: Set hyssop, and weed up thyme: Supply
10 it with one gender of herbs, or distract it with many: either to have it sterile with idleness, or manur'd with industry, why the power, and corrigible authority of this lies in our wills. If the brain of our lives had not one scale of reason, to poise another of sensuality, the blood,
15 and baseness of our natures would conduct us to most prepost'rous conclusions. But we have reason to cool our raging motions, our carnal stings, or unbitted lusts: whereof I take this, that you call love, to be a sect, or scion.

20 RODERIGO: It cannot be.

IAGO: It is merely a lust of the blood, and a permission of the will. Come, be a man: drown thyself? Drown cats, and blind puppies. I have profess'd me thy friend, and I confess me knit to thy deserving, with cables of
25 perdurable toughness. I could never better stead thee than now. Put money in thy purse: follow thou the wars, defeat thy favour, with an usurp'd beard. I say put money in thy purse. It cannot be long that Desdemona should continue her love to the Moor. Put money in thy
30 purse: nor he his to her. It was a violent commencement in her, and thou shalt see an answerable sequestration, put but money in thy purse. These Moors are changeable in their wills: fill thy purse with money. The food

that to him now is as luscious as locusts, shall be to him shortly, as bitter as coloquintida. She must change for youth: when she is sated with his body she will find the errors of her choice. Therefore, put money in thy purse. If thou wilt needs damn thyself, do it a more delicate 5 way than drowning. Make all the money thou canst: If sanctimony, and a frail vow, betwixt an erring barbarian, and super-subtle Venetian be not too hard for my wits, and all the tribe of hell, thou shalt enjoy her: therefore make money: a pox of drowning thyself, it is 10 clean out of the way. Seek thou rather to be hang'd in compassing thy joy, than to be drown'd, and go without her.

RODERIGO: Wilt thou be fast to my hopes, if I depend on the issue? 15

IAGO: Thou art sure of me: go make money: I have told thee often, and I retell thee again, and again, I hate the Moor. My cause is hearted; thine hath no less reason. Let us be conjunctive in our revenge, against him. If thou canst cuckold him, thou dost thyself a pleasure, 20 and me a sport. There are many events in the womb of Time, which will be delivered. Traverse, go, provide thy money. We will have more of this tomorrow. Adieu.

RODERIGO: Where shall we meet i' th' morning? 25
IAGO: At my lodging.
RODERIGO: I 'll be with thee betimes.
IAGO: Go to, farewell. Do you hear Roderigo?
RODERIGO: I 'll sell all my land.

Exit. 30

IAGO: Thus do I ever make my fool, my purse:
For I mine own gain'd knowledge should profane
If I would time expend with such a snipe,

But for my sport, and profit: I hate the Moor,
And it is thought abroad, that 'twixt my sheets
He 's done my office. I know not if 't be true,
But I, for mere suspicion in that kind,
5   Will do, as if for surety. He holds me well,
The better shall my purpose work on him:
Cassio 's a proper man: Let me see now,
To get his place, and to plume up my will
In double knavery. How? How? Let 's see.
10   After some time, to abuse Othello's ears,
That he is too familiar with his wife:
He hath a person, and a smooth dispose
To be suspected: fram'd to make women false.
The Moor is of a free, and open nature,
15   That thinks men honest, that but seem to be so,
And will as tenderly be led by th' nose
As asses are:
I have 't: it is engender'd: Hell, and Night,
Must bring this monstrous birth, to the world's light.
20   *Exit.*

II. 1

Enter Montano, Governor of Cyprus, and two
Gentlemen.

MONTANO: What from the Cape, can you discern at sea?
25 I GENTLEMAN: Nothing at all, it is a high wrought flood:
I cannot 'twixt the heaven, and the main,
Descry a sail.
MONTANO: Methinks, the wind hath spoke aloud at land,
A fuller blast ne'er shook our battlements:
30   If it hath ruffian'd so upon the sea,
What ribs of oak, when the mountains melt on them,

Can hold the mortise. What shall we hear of this?
2 GENTLEMAN: A segregation of the Turkish Fleet:
For do but stand upon the foaming shore,
The chidden billow seems to pelt the clouds,
The wind-shak'd surge, with high and monstrous main   5
Seems to cast water on the burning Bear,
And quench the guards of th' ever-fixed Pole:
I never did like molestation view
On the enchafed flood.
MONTANO: If that the Turkish Fleet   10
Be not enshelter'd, and embay'd, they are drown'd,
It is impossible to bear it out.
Enter a Gentleman.
3 GENTLEMAN: News Lads: our wars are done:
The desperate tempest hath so bang'd the Turks,   15
That their designment halts. A noble ship of Venice,
Hath seen a grievous wrack and sufferance
On most part of their fleet.
MONTANO: How? Is this true?
3 GENTLEMAN: The ship is here put in: a Veronesa, 20
  Michael Cassio
Lieutenant to the warlike Moor, Othello,
Is come on shore: the Moor himself at sea,
And is in full commission here for Cyprus.
MONTANO: I am glad on 't: 25
'Tis a worthy Governor.
3 GENTLEMAN: But this same Cassio, though he speak of
  comfort,
Touching the Turkish loss, yet he looks sadly,
And prays the Moor be safe; for they were parted   30
With foul and violent tempest.
MONTANO: Pray Heavens he be:
For I have serv'd him, and the man commands

Like a full soldier. Let 's to the seaside (hoa)
As well to see the vessel that 's come in,
As to throw out our eyes for brave Othello,
Even till we make the main, and th' aerial blue,
5   An indistinct regard.

3 GENTLEMAN: Come, let 's do so;
For every minute is expectancy
Of more arrivance.

Enter Cassio.

10 CASSIO: Thanks, you the valiant of the warlike Isle,
That so approve the Moor: Oh let the Heavens
Give him defence against the elements,
For I have lost him on a dangerous sea.

MONTANO: Is he well shipp'd?

15 CASSIO: His bark is stoutly timber'd, and his pilot
Of very expert, and approv'd allowance;
Therefore my hopes (not surfeited to death)
Stand in bold cure.

WITHIN: A sail, a sail, a sail.

20 CASSIO: What noise?

2 GENTLEMAN: The Town is empty; on the brow o' th'
sea
Stand ranks of people, and they cry, a sail.

CASSIO: My hopes do shape him for the Governor. *A shot.*

25 2 GENTLEMAN: They do discharge their shot of courtesy,
Our friends, at least.

CASSIO: I pray you Sir, go forth,
And give us truth who 'tis that is arriv'd.

2 GENTLEMAN: I shall.   *Exit.*

30 MONTANO: But good Lieutenant, is your General wiv'd?

CASSIO: Most fortunately: he hath achiev'd a Maid
That paragons description, and wild fame:
One that excels the quirks of blazoning pens,

And in th' essential vesture of creation,
Does tire the ingeniver.

Enter Gentleman.

How now? Who has put in?

2 GENTLEMAN: 'Tis one Iago, Ancient to the General.　5

CASSIO: Ha's had most favourable, and happy speed:
Tempests themselves, high seas, and howling winds,
The gutter'd rocks, and congregated sands,
Traitors ensteep'd, to enclog the guiltless keel,
As having sense of beauty, do omit　　　　　　　10
Their mortal natures, letting go safely by
The divine Desdemona.

MONTANO: What is she?

CASSIO: She that I spake of:
Our great Captain's Captain,　　　　　　　　　15
Left in the conduct of the bold Iago,
Whose footing here anticipates our thoughts,
A sennight's speed. Great Jove, Othello guard,
And swell his sail with thine own powerful breath,
That he may bless this Bay with his tall ship,　　20
Make love's quick pants in Desdemona's arms,
Give renew'd fire to our extincted spirits.

Enter Desdemona, Iago, Roderigo, and Emilia.

Oh behold,
The riches of the ship is come on shore:　　　　25
You men of Cyprus, let her have your knees.
Hail to thee Lady: and the grace of Heaven,
Before, behind thee, and on every hand
Enwheel thee round.

DESDEMONA: I thank you, valiant Cassio,　　　30
What tidings can you tell me of my Lord?

CASSIO: He is not yet arriv'd, nor know I aught
But that he 's well, and will be shortly here.

DESDEMONA; Oh, but I fear:
How lost you company?

CASSIO: The great contention of sea, and skies
Parted our fellowship. But hark, a sail.

5 WITHIN: A sail, a sail.

2 GENTLEMAN: They give this greeting to the Citadel:
This likewise is a friend.

CASSIO: See for the news:
Good Ancient, you are welcome. Welcome Mistress:
10   Let it not gall your patience (good Iago)
That I extend my manners. 'Tis my breeding,
That gives me this bold show of courtesy.

IAGO: Sir, would she give you so much of her lips,
As of her tongue she oft bestows on me,
15   You would have enough.

DESDEMONA: Alas: she has no speech.

IAGO: In faith too much:
I find it still, when I have leave to sleep.
Marry before your Ladyship, I grant,
20   She puts her tongue a little in her heart,
And chides with thinking.

EMILIA: You have little cause to say so.

IAGO: Come on, come on: you are pictures out of door:
bells in your parlours: wild-cats in your kitchens:
25   saints in your injuries: devils being offended: players
in your housewifery, and housewives in your beds.

DESDEMONA: Oh, fie upon thee, slanderer.

IAGO: Nay, it is true: or else I am a Turk,
You rise to play, and go to bed to work.

30 EMILIA: You shall not write my praise.

IAGO: No, let me not.

DESDEMONA: What wouldst write of me, if thou shouldst
praise me?

IAGO: Oh, gentle Lady, do not put me to 't,
For I am nothing, if not critical.

DESDEMONA: Come on, assay.
There 's one gone to the Harbour?

IAGO: Ay Madam.

DESDEMONA: I am not merry: but I do beguile
The thing I am, by seeming otherwise.
Come, how wouldst thou praise me?

IAGO: I am about it, but indeed my invention comes
from my pate, as birdlime does from freeze, it plucks
out brains and all. But my Muse labours, and thus she
is deliver'd.
If she be fair, and wise: fairness, and wit,
The one 's for use, the other useth it.

DESDEMONA: Well prais'd:
How if she be black and witty?

IAGO: *If she be black, and thereto have a wit,*
She 'll find a white, that shall her blackness fit.

DESDEMONA: Worse, and worse.

EMILIA: How if fair and foolish?

IAGO: *She never yet was foolish that was fair,*
For even her folly help'd her to an heir.

DESDEMONA: These are old fond paradoxes, to make
fools laugh i' th' alehouse. What miserable praise hast
thou for her that's foul, and foolish.

IAGO: *There 's none so foul and foolish thereunto,*
But does foul pranks, which fair, and wise ones do.

DESDEMONA: Oh heavy ignorance: thou praisest the
worst best. But what praise couldst thou bestow on
a deserving woman indeed? One, that in the authority
of her merit, did justly put on the vouch of very malice
itself.

IAGO: *She that was ever fair, and never proud,*

Had tongue at will, and yet was never loud:
Never lack'd gold, and yet went never gay,
Fled from her wish, and yet said now I may.
She that being anger'd, her revenge being nigh,
5   *Bad her wrong stay, and her displeasure fly:*
She that in wisdom never was so frail,
To change the cod's head for the salmon's tail:
She that could think, and ne'er disclose her mind,
See suitors following, and not look behind:
10   *She was a wight, (if ever such wights were)*

DESDEMONA: To do what?

IAGO: *To suckle fools, and chronicle small beer.*

DESDEMONA: Oh most lame and impotent conclusion.
Do not learn of him Emilia, though he be thy husband.
15   How say you (Cassio) is he not a most profane, and
liberal counsellor?

CASSIO: He speaks home (Madam) you may relish him
more in the soldier, than in the scholar.

IAGO: He takes her by the palm: ay, well said, whisper.
20   With as little a web as this, will I ensnare as great a fly as
Cassio. Ay smile upon her, do: I will give thee in thine
own courtship. You say true, 'tis so indeed. If such tricks
as these strip you out of your lieutenantry, it had been
better you had not kiss'd your three fingers so oft,
25   which now again you are most apt to play the Sir, in.
Very good: well kiss'd, and excellent courtesy: 'tis so
indeed. Yet again, your fingers to your lips? Would
they were clyster-pipes for your sake. [*Trumpets within.*]
The Moor. I know his trumpet.

30   CASSIO: 'Tis truly so.

DESDEMONA: Let's meet him, and receive him.

CASSIO: Lo, where he comes.

                    Enter Othello, and Attendants.

OTHELLO: O, my fair warrior.

DESDEMONA: My dear Othello.

OTHELLO: It gives me wonder, great as my content
To see you here before me.
Oh my soul's joy: 5
If after every tempest, come such calms,
May the winds blow, till they have waken'd death:
And let the labouring bark climb hills of seas
Olympus high: and duck again as low,
As hell's from Heaven. If it were now to die,   10
'Twere now to be most happy. For I fear,
My soul hath her content so absolute,
That not another comfort like to this,
Succeeds in unknown fate.

DESDEMONA: The Heavens forbid   15
But that our loves
And comforts should increase
Even as our days do grow.

OTHELLO: Amen to that (sweet Powers)
I cannot speak enough of this content,   20
It stops me here: it is too much of joy.
And this, and this the greatest discords be   *They kiss.*
That e'er our hearts shall make.

IAGO: Oh you are well tun'd now: But I'll set down the
pegs that make this music, as honest as I am.   25

OTHELLO: Come: let us to the Castle.
News (Friends) our wars are done:
The Turks are drown'd.
How does my old acquaintance of this Isle?
(Honey) you shall be well desir'd in Cyprus,   30
I have found great love amongst them. Oh my Sweet,
I prattle out of fashion, and I dote
In mine own comforts. I prithee, good Iago,

Go to the Bay, and disembark my coffers:
Bring thou the Master to the Citadel,
He is a good one, and his worthiness
Does challenge much respect. Come, Desdemona,
5   Once more well met at Cyprus.
                    Exeunt Othello and Desdemona.
IAGO: Do thou meet me presently at the Harbour. Come
    thither, if thou be'st valiant, (as they say base men
    being in love, have then a nobility in their natures,
10 . more than is native to them) list me; the Lieutenant
    tonight watches on the Court of Guard. First, I must tell
    thee this: Desdemona, is directly in love with him.
RODERIGO: With him? Why, 'tis not possible.
IAGO: Lay thy finger thus: and let thy soul be instructed.
15   Mark me with what violence she first lov'd the Moor,
    but for bragging, and telling her fantastical lies. To love
    him still for prating, let not thy discreet heart think it.
    Her eye must be fed. And what delight shall she have to
    look on the devil? When the blood is made dull with the
20   act of sport, there should be a game to inflame it, and
    to give satiety a fresh appetite. Loveliness in favour,
    sympathy in years, manners, and beauties: all which the
    Moor is defective in. Now for want of these requir'd
    conveniences, her delicate tenderness will find itself
25   abus'd, begin to heave the gorge, disrelish and abhor
    the Moor, very Nature will instruct her in it, and com-
    pel her to some second choice. Now Sir, this granted (as
    it is a most pregnant and unforc'd position) who stands
    so eminent in the degree of this fortune, as Cassio does: a
30   knave very voluble: no further conscionable, than in
    putting on the mere form of civil, and humane seeming,
    for the better compass of his salt, and most hidden loose
    affection? Why none, why none: A slipper, and subtle

knave, a finder of occasion: that he's an eye can stamp, and counterfeit advantages, though true advantage never present itself. A devilish knave: besides, the knave is handsome, young: and hath all those requisites in him, that folly and green minds look after. A pestilent 5 complete knave, and the woman hath found him already.

RODERIGO: I cannot believe that in her, she's full of most bless'd condition.

IAGO: Bless'd fig's end. The wine she drinks is made of grapes. If she had been bless'd, she would never have 10 lov'd the Moor: Bless'd pudding. Didst thou not see her paddle with the palm of his hand? Didst not mark that?

RODERIGO: Yes, that I did: but that was but courtesy.

IAGO: Lechery by this hand: an index, and obscure pro- logue to the history of lust and foul thoughts. They met 15 so near with their lips, that their breaths embrac'd together. Villainous thoughts Roderigo, when these mutabilities so marshal the way, hard at hand comes the master, and main exercise, th' incorporate conclusion: Pish. But Sir, be you rul'd by me. I have brought you 20 from Venice. Watch you tonight: for the command, I'll lay 't upon you. Cassio knows you not: I'll not be far from you. Do you find some occasion to anger Cassio, either by speaking too loud, or tainting his discipline, or from what other course you please, which the time shall 25 more favourably minister.

RODERIGO: Well.

IAGO: Sir, he's rash, and very sudden in choler: and haply may strike at you, provoke him that he may: for even out of that will I cause these of Cyprus to 30 mutiny. Whose qualification shall come into no true taste again, but by the displanting of Cassio. So shall you have a shorter journey to your desires, by the means

I shall then have to prefer them. And the impediment most profitably removed, without the which there were no expectation of our prosperity.

RODERIGO: I will do this, if you can bring it to any
5   opportunity.

IAGO: I warrant thee. Meet me by and by at the Citadel. I must fetch his necessaries ashore. Farewell.

RODERIGO: Adieu. *Exit.*

IAGO: That Cassio loves her, I do well believe 't:
10   That she loves him, 'tis apt, and of great credit.
    The Moor (howbeit that I endure him not)
    Is of a constant, loving, noble nature,
    And I dare think, he 'll prove to Desdemona
    A most dear·husband. Now I do love her too,
15   Not out of absolute lust, (though peradventure
    I stand accomptant for as great a sin)
    But partly led to diet my revenge,
    For that I do suspect the lusty Moor
    Hath leap'd into my seat. The thought whereof,
20   Doth (like a poisonous mineral) gnaw my inwards:
    And nothing can, or shall content my soul
    Till I am even'd with him, wife, for wife.
    Or failing so, yet that I put the Moor,
    At least into a jealousy so strong
25   That judgement cannot cure. Which thing to do,
    If this poor Trash of Venice, whom I trace
    For his quick hunting, stand the putting on,
    I 'll have our Michael Cassio on the hip,
    Abuse him to the Moor, in the right garb
30   (For I fear Cassio with my night-cap too)
    Make the Moor thank me, love me, and reward me,
    For making him egregiously an ass,
    And practising upon his peace, and quiet,

Even to madness. 'Tis here: but yet confus'd,
Knavery's plain face, is never seen, till us'd.
Exit.

II.2

Enter Othello's Herald with a proclamation. 5

HERALD: It is Othello's pleasure, our noble and valiant
General. That upon certain tidings now arriv'd, im-
porting the mere perdition of the Turkish Fleet: every
man put himself into triumph. Some to dance, some to
make bonfires, each man, to what sport and revels his 10
addition leads him. For besides these beneficial news, it
is the celebration of his nuptial. So much was his pleasure
should be proclaimed. All offices are open, and there is
full liberty of feasting from this present hour of five, till
the bell hath told eleven. Heaven bless the Isle of Cyprus, 15
and our noble General Othello.
Exit.
Enter Othello, Desdemona, Cassio, and Attendants.

OTHELLO: Good Michael, look you to the guard tonight.
Let's teach ourselves that honourable stop,   20
Not to out-sport discretion.

CASSIO: Iago hath direction what to do.
But notwithstanding with my personal eye
Will I look to 't.

OTHELLO: Iago is most honest: 25
Michael, good night. Tomorrow with your earliest,
Let me have speech with you. Come my dear Love,
The purchase made, the fruits are to ensue,
That profit 's yet to come 'tween me, and you.
Good night.   30
Exeunt Othello, Desdemona, and Attendants.

Enter Iago.

CASSIO: Welcome Iago: we must to the watch.

IAGO: Not this hour Lieutenant: 'tis not yet ten o' th'
     clock. Our General cast us thus early for the love of his
5   Desdemona: Who, let us not therefore blame; he hath
     not yet made wanton the night with her: and she is
     sport for Jove.

CASSIO: She's a most exquisite Lady.

IAGO: And I'll warrant her, full of game.

10   CASSIO: Indeed she is a most fresh and delicate creature.

IAGO: What an eye she has?
     Methinks it sounds a parley to provocation.

CASSIO: An inviting eye:
     And yet methinks right modest.

15   IAGO: And when she speaks,
     Is it not an alarum to Love?

CASSIO: She is indeed perfection.

IAGO: Well: happiness to their sheets. Come Lieutenant,
     I have a stoup of wine, and here without are a brace of
20   Cyprus Gallants, that would fain have a measure to the
     health of black Othello.

CASSIO: Not tonight, good Iago, I have very poor, and
     unhappy brains for drinking. I could well wish courtesy
     would invent some other custom of entertainment.

25   IAGO: Oh, they are our friends: but one cup, I'll drink for
     you.

CASSIO: I have drunk but one cup tonight, and that was
     craftily qualified too: and behold what innovation it
     makes here. I am infortunate in the infirmity, and dare
30   not task my weakness with any more.

IAGO: What man? 'Tis a night of revels, the Gallants
     desire it.

CASSIO: Where are they?

IAGO: Here, at the door: I pray you call them in.

CASSIO: I 'll do 't, but it dislikes me. *Exit.*

IAGO: If I can fasten but one cup upon him
 With that which he hath drunk tonight already,
 He'll be as full of quarrel, and offence   5
 As my young Mistress' dog.
 Now my sick fool Roderigo,
 Whom Love hath turn'd almost the wrong side out,
 To Desdemona hath tonight carous'd,
 Potations, pottle-deep; and he 's to watch.   10
 Three else of Cyprus, noble swelling spirits,
 (That hold their honours in a wary distance,
 The very elements of this warlike Isle)
 Have I tonight fluster'd with flowing cups,
 And they watch too.   15
 Now 'mongst this flock of drunkards
 Am I to put our Cassio in some action
 That may offend the Isle. But here they come.
   Enter Cassio, Montano, and Gentlemen.
 If consequence do but approve my dream,   20
 My boat sails freely, both with wind and stream.

CASSIO: 'Fore God, they have given me a rouse already.

MONTANO: Good faith a little one: not past a pint, as I
 am a soldier.

IAGO: Some wine hoa.   25
   And let me the canakin clink, clink:
   And let me the canakin clink.
   A soldier's a man: Oh, man's life 's but a span,
   Why then let a soldier drink.
 Some wine boys.   30

CASSIO: 'Fore God: an excellent song.

IAGO: I learn'd it in England: where indeed they are
 most potent in potting. Your Dane, your German,

and your swag-belli'd Hollander (drink hoa) are nothing to your English.

CASSIO: Is your Englishmen so exquisite in his drinking?

IAGO: Why, he drinks you with facility, your Dane dead
5 drunk. He sweats not to overthrow your Almain. He gives your Hollander a vomit, ere the next pottle can be fill'd.

CASSIO: To the health of our General.

MONTANO: I am for it Lieutenant: and I 'll do you justice.

10 IAGO: Oh sweet England.

> *King Stephen was and a worthy peer,*
> *His breeches cost him but a crown,*
> *He held them sixpence all too dear,*
> *With that he call'd the tailor lown:*
15 > *He was a wight of high renown,*
> *And thou art but of low degree:*
> *'Tis pride that pulls the country down,*
> *Then take thy auld cloak about thee.*

Some wine hoa.

20 CASSIO: 'Fore God, this is a more exquisite song than the other.

IAGO: Will you hear 't again?

CASSIO: No: for I hold him to be unworthy of his place, that does those things. Well: God 's above all: and
25 there be souls must be saved, and there be souls must not be saved.

IAGO: It is true, good Lieutenant.

CASSIO: For mine own part, no offence to the General, nor any man of quality: I hope to be saved.

30 IAGO: And so do I too Lieutenant.

CASSIO: Ay: (but by your leave) not before me. The Lieutenant is to be saved before the Ancient. Let 's have no more of this: let 's to our affairs. God forgive

us our sins: Gentlemen let 's look to our business. Do
not think Gentlemen, I am drunk: this is my Ancient,
this is my right hand, and this is my left. I am not drunk
now: I can stand well enough, and I speak well enough.

GENTLEMEN: Excellent well.   5

CASSIO: Why very well then: you must not think then,
that I am drunk.   *Exit.*

MONTANO: To th' platform (Masters) come, let 's set the
watch.

IAGO: You see this fellow, that is gone before,   10
He is a soldier, fit to stand by Caesar,
And give direction. And do but see his vice,
'Tis to his virtue, a just equinox,
The one as long as th' other. 'Tis pity of him:
I fear the trust Othello puts him in,   15
On some odd time of his infirmity
Will shake this Island.

MONTANO: But is he often thus?

IAGO: 'Tis evermore his prologue to his sleep,
He 'll watch the horologe a double set,   20
If drink rock not his cradle.

MONTANO: It were well
The General were put in mind of it:
Perhaps he sees it not, or his good nature
Prizes the virtue that appears in Cassio,   25
And looks not on his evils: is not this true?
                    Enter Roderigo.

IAGO: How now Roderigo?
I pray you after the Lieutenant, go.
                    Exit Roderigo.   30

MONTANO: And 'tis great pity, that the noble Moor
Should hazard such a place, as his own second
With one of an ingraft infirmity;

It were an honest action, to say so
To the Moor.

IAGO: Not I, for this fair Island,
I do love Cassio well: and would do much
5   *Within*: Help, help.
To cure him of his evil. But hark what noise?
              Enter Cassio, pursuing Roderigo.

CASSIO: 'Zounds, you rogue: you rascal.

MONTANO: What's the matter Lieutenant?

10 CASSIO: A knave teach me my duty? I'll beat the knave
into a twiggen bottle.

RODERIGO: Beat me?

CASSIO: Dost thou prate, Rogue?

MONTANO: Nay, good Lieutenant:
15   I pray you Sir, hold your hand.

CASSIO: Let me go (Sir)
Or I'll knock you o'er the mazzard.

MONTANO: Come, come: you're drunk.

CASSIO: Drunk?
20   *They fight.*

IAGO: Away I say: go out and cry a mutiny.
              Exit Roderigo. A bell rung.
Nay good Lieutenant. God's will Gentlemen:
Help hoa. Lieutenant. Sir Montano:
25   Help Masters. Here's a goodly watch indeed.
Who's that which rings the bell. Diablo, hoa:
The Town will rise. God's will Lieutenant,
You will be asham'd for ever.
              Enter Othello, and Attendants with weapons.

30 OTHELLO: What is the matter here?

MONTANO: 'Zounds, I bleed still, I am hurt to th' death.

OTHELLO: Hold for your lives.

IAGO: Hold hoa. Lieutenant, Sir Montano, Gentlemen:

Have you forgot all sense of place and duty?
Hold. The General speaks to you: hold for shame.

OTHELLO: Why how now hoa? From whence ariseth
   this?
  Are we turn'd Turks? and to ourselves do that   5
  Which Heaven hath forbid the Ottomites.
  For Christian shame, put by this barbarous brawl:
  He that stirs next, to carve for his own rage,
  Holds his soul light: He dies upon his motion.
  Silence that dreadful bell, it frights the Isle,   10
  From her propriety. What is the matter, Masters?
  Honest Iago that looks dead with grieving,
  Speak: who began this? On thy love I charge thee.

IAGO: I do not know: friends all, but now, even now.
  In quarter, and in terms like bride, and groom   15
  Devesting them for bed: and then, but now:
  (As if some planet had unwitted men)
  Swords out, and tilting one at other's breasts,
  In opposition bloody. I cannot speak
  Any beginning to this peevish odds.   20
  And would, in action glorious, I had lost
  Those legs, that brought me to a part of it.

OTHELLO: How comes it (Michael) you are thus forgot?

CASSIO: I pray you pardon me, I cannot speak.

OTHELLO: Worthy Montano, you were wont to be civil: 25
  The gravity, and stillness of your youth
  The world hath noted. And your name is great
  In mouths of wisest censure. What's the matter
  That you unlace your reputation thus,
  And spend your rich opinion, for the name   30
  Of a night-brawler? Give me answer to it.

MONTANO: Worthy Othello, I am hurt to danger,
  Your officer Iago, can inform you,

While I spare speech which something now offends me.
Of all that I do know, nor know I aught
By me, that's said, or done amiss this night,
Unless self-charity be sometimes a vice,
5   And to defend ourselves, it be a sin
When violence assails us.

OTHELLO: Now by Heaven,
My blood begins my safer guides to rule,
And passion (having my best judgement collied)
10   Assays to lead the way. Zounds if I stir,
Or do but lift this arm, the best of you
Shall sink in my rebuke. Give me to know
How this foul rout began: Who set it on,
And he that is approv'd in this offence,
15   Though he had twinn'd with me, both at a birth,
Shall lose me. What in a town of war,
Yet wild, the people's hearts brim-full of fear,
To manage private, and domestic quarrel?
In night, and on the Court and Guard of safety?
20   'Tis monstrous: Iago, who began 't?

MONTANO: If partially affin'd, or leagu'd in office,
Thou dost deliver more, or less than truth,
Thou art no soldier.

IAGO: Touch me not so near,
25   I had rather have this tongue cut from my mouth,
Than it should do offence to Michael Cassio.
Yet I persuade myself, to speak the truth,
Shall nothing wrong him. This it is General:
Montano and myself being in speech,
30   There comes a fellow crying out for help,
And Cassio following him with determin'd sword
To execute upon him. Sir, this Gentleman,
Steps in to Cassio, and entreats his pause:

Myself, the crying fellow did pursue,
Lest by his clamour (as it so fell out)
The Town might fall in fright. He, (swift of foot)
Out-ran my purpose: and I return'd then rather
For that I heard the clink, and fall of swords,   5
And Cassio high in oath: Which till tonight
I ne'er might say before. When I came back
(For this was brief) I found them close together
At blow, and thrust, even as again they were
When you yourself did part them.   10
More of this matter cannot I report,
But men are men: the best sometimes forget,
Though Cassio did some little wrong to him,
As men in rage strike those that wish them best,
Yet surely Cassio I believe receiv'd   15
From him that fled, some strange indignity,
Which patience could not pass.
OTHELLO: I know Iago
Thy honesty, and love doth mince this matter,
Making it light to Cassio: Cassio, I love thee,   20
But never more be Officer of mine.
              Enter Desdemona attended.
Look if my gentle Love be not rais'd up:
I'll make thee an example.
DESDEMONA: What is the matter (dear)?   25
OTHELLO: All's well, Sweeting:
Come away to bed. Sir for your hurts,
Myself will be your surgeon. Lead him off:
Iago, look with care about the Town,
And silence those whom this vile brawl distracted.   30
Come Desdemona, 'tis the soldiers' life,
To have their balmy slumbers wak'd with strife.
              Exeunt all but Iago and Cassio.

IAGO: What are you hurt Lieutenant?

CASSIO: Ay, past all surgery.

IAGO: Marry God forbid.

CASSIO: Reputation, reputation, reputation: Oh I have
5 lost my reputation. I have lost the immortal part of
myself, and what remains is bestial. My reputation, Iago,
my reputation.

IAGO: As I am an honest man I had thought you had
received some bodily wound; there is more sense in
10 that than in reputation. Reputation is an idle, and most
false imposition; oft got without merit, and lost without deserving. You have lost no reputation at all, unless
you repute yourself such a loser. What man, there are
more ways to recover the General again. You are but
15 now cast in his mood, (a punishment more in policy,
than in malice) even so as one would beat his offenceless
dog, to affright an imperious lion. Sue to him again,
and he 's yours.

CASSIO: I will rather sue to be despis'd, than to deceive
20 so good a Commander, with so slight, so drunken, and
so indiscreet an Officer. Drunk? And speak parrot?
And squabble? Swagger? Swear? And discourse fustian
with one's own shadow? Oh thou invisible spirit of
wine, if thou hast no name to be known by, let us call
25 thee devil.

IAGO: What was he that you follow'd with your sword?
What had he done to you?

CASSIO: I know not.

IAGO: Is 't possible?

30 CASSIO: I remember a mass of things, but nothing distinctly: a quarrel, but nothing wherefore. Oh God,
that men should put an enemy in their mouths, to steal
away their brains? that we should with joy, pleasance,

revel and applause, transform ourselves into beasts.

IAGO: Why? But you are now well enough: how came
you thus recovered?

CASSIO: It hath pleas'd the devil drunkenness, to give
place to the devil wrath, one unperfectness, shows me   5
another to make me frankly despise myself.

IAGO: Come, you are too severe a moraler. As the time,
the place, and the condition of this Country stands
I could heartily wish this had not befallen: but since it is,
as it is, mend it for your own good.   10

CASSIO: I will ask him for my place again, he shall tell
me, I am a drunkard: had I as many mouths as Hydra,
such an answer would stop them all. To be now a sen-
sible man, by and by a fool, and presently a beast. Oh
strange! Every inordinate cup is unbless'd, and the   15
ingredient is a devil.

IAGO: Come, come: good wine, is a good familiar
creature, if it be well us'd: exclaim no more against it.
And good Lieutenant, I think, you think I love you.

CASSIO: I have well approved it, Sir. I drunk?   20

IAGO: You, or any man living, may be drunk at a time
man. I tell you what you shall do: Our General's wife,
is now the General. I may say so, in this respect, for that
he hath devoted, and given up himself to the contem-
plation, mark: and the devotement of her parts and   25
graces. Confess yourself freely to her: Importune her
help to put you in your place again. She is of so free, so
kind, so apt, so blessed a disposition, she holds it a vice
in her goodness, not to do more than she is requested.
This broken joint between you, and her husband, en-   30
treat her to splinter. And my fortunes against any lay
worth naming, this crack of your love, shall grow
stronger, than it was before.

CASSIO: You advise me well.

IAGO: I protest in the sincerity of Love, and honest
kindness.

CASSIO: I think it freely: and betimes in the morning,
5   I will beseech the virtuous Desdemona to undertake for
me: I am desperate of my fortunes if they check me.

IAGO: You are in the right: good night Lieutenant, I must
to the watch.

CASSIO: Good night, honest Iago.
10   *Exit Cassio.*

IAGO: And what's he then,
That says I play the villain?
When this advice is free I give, and honest,
Probal to thinking, and indeed the course
15   To win the Moor again.
For 'tis most easy
Th' inclining Desdemona to subdue
In any honest suit. She's fram'd as fruitful
As the free elements. And then for her
20   To win the Moor, were to renounce his baptism,
All seals, and symbols of redeemed sin:
His soul is so infetter'd to her love,
That she may make, unmake, do what she list,
Even as her appetite shall play the god,
25   With his weak function. How am I then a villain,
To counsel Cassio to this parallel course,
Directly to his good? Divinity of hell,
When devils will the blackest sins put on,
They do suggest at first with heavenly shows,
30   As I do now. For whiles this honest fool
Plies Desdemona, to repair his fortune,
And she for him, pleads strongly to the Moor,
I'll pour this pestilence into his ear:

That she repeals him, for her body's lust,
And by how much she strives to do him good,
She shall undo her credit with the Moor.
So will I turn her virtue into pitch,
And out of her own goodness make the net,   5
That shall enmesh them all.
How now Roderigo?
Enter Roderigo.

RODERIGO: I do follow here in the chase, not like a
hound that hunts, but one that fills up the cry. My   10
money is almost spent; I have been tonight exceedingly
well cudgel'd: And I think the issue will be, I shall have
so much experience for my pains; And so, with no
money at all, and a little more wit, return again to
Venice.   15

IAGO: How poor are they that have not patience?
What wound did ever heal but by degrees?
Thou know'st we work by wit, and not by witchcraft,
And wit depends on dilatory time:
Does't not go well? Cassio hath beaten thee,   20
And thou by that small hurt hath cashier'd Cassio:
Though other things grow fair against the Sun,
Yet fruits that blossom first, will first be ripe:
Content thyself, awhile. By the mass, 'tis morning;
Pleasure, and action, make the hours seem short.   25
Retire thee, go where thou art billeted:
Away, I say, thou shalt know more hereafter:
Nay get thee gone.   *Exit Roderigo.*
Two things are to be done:
My wife must move for Cassio to her Mistress: 30
I'll set her on myself, a while, to draw the Moor apart,
And bring him jump, when he may Cassio find
Soliciting his wife: ay, that's the way:

Dull not device, by coldness, and delay.
Exit.

III. 1

Enter Cassio, Musicians, and Clown.

5 CASSIO: Masters, play here, I will content your pains,
   Something that's brief: and bid, good morrow General.

   CLOWN: Why Masters, have your instruments been in
   Naples, that they speak i' th' nose thus?

   MUSICIAN: How sir? how?

10 CLOWN: Are these I pray you, wind instruments?

   MUSICIAN: Ay marry are they sir.

   CLOWN: Oh, thereby hangs a tale.

   MUSICIAN: Whereby hangs a tale, sir?

   CLOWN: Marry sir, by many a wind instrument that I
15 know. But Masters, here 's money for you: and the
   General so likes your music, that he desires you for
   love's sake to make no more noise with it.

   MUSICIAN: Well Sir, we will not.

   CLOWN: If you have any music that may not be heard,
20 to 't again. But (as they say) to hear music, the General
   does not greatly care.

   MUSICIAN: We have none such, sir.

   CLOWN: Then put up your pipes in your bag, for I 'll
   away. Go, vanish into air, away.
25   *Exeunt Musicians.*

   CASSIO: Dost thou hear me, mine honest friend?

   CLOWN: No, I hear not your honest friend: I hear you.

   CASSIO: Prithee keep up thy quillets, there 's a poor piece
   of gold for thee: if the Gentlewoman that attends
30 the General be stirring, tell her, there 's one Cassio
   entreats her a little favour of speech. Wilt thou do this?

CLOWN: She is stirring sir: if she will stir hither, I shall
seem to notify unto her.

CASSIO: Do, good my friend.

Exit Clown.

Enter Iago.   5

In happy time, Iago.

IAGO: You have not been a-bed then?

CASSIO: Why no: the day had broke before we parted.
I have made bold (Iago) to send in to your wife;
My suit to her is, that she will to virtuous Desdemona   10
Procure me some access.

IAGO: I'll send her to you presently:
And I'll devise a mean to draw the Moor
Out of the way, that your converse and business
May be more free.   *Exit.*   15

CASSIO: I humbly thank you for 't. I never knew
A Florentine more kind, and honest.

Enter Emilia.

EMILIA: Good morrow (good Lieutenant) I am sorry
For your displeasure: but all will sure be well.   20
The General and his wife are talking of it,
And she speaks for you stoutly. The Moor replies,
That he you hurt is of great fame in Cyprus,
And great affinity: and that in wholesome wisdom
He might not but refuse you. But he protests he loves   25
you
And needs no other suitor, but his likings
To take the safest occasion by the front
To bring you in again.

CASSIO: Yet I beseech you,   30
If you think fit, or that it may be done,
Give me advantage of some brief discourse
With Desdemon alone.

EMILIA: Pray you come in:
   I will bestow you where you shall have time
   To speak your bosom freely.
CASSIO: I am much bound to you.
5   *Exeunt.*

III. 2

Enter Othello, Iago, and Gentlemen.
OTHELLO: These letters give (Iago) to the Pilot,
   And by him do my duties to the Senate:
10   That done, I will be walking on the works,
   Repair there to me.
IAGO: Well, my good Lord, I 'll do 't.
OTHELLO: This fortification (Gentlemen) shall we see 't?
GENTLEMEN: We'll await upon your Lordship.
15   *Exeunt.*

III. 3

Enter Desdemona, Cassio, and Emilia.
DESDEMONA: Be thou assur'd (good Cassio) I will do
   All my abilities in thy behalf.
20 EMILIA: Good Madam do:
   I warrant it grieves my husband,
   As if the cause were his.
DESDEMONA: Oh that 's an honest fellow: Do not doubt
      Cassio
25 But I will have my Lord, and you again
   As friendly as you were.
CASSIO: Bounteous Madam,
   Whatever shall become of Michael Cassio,
   He 's never anything but your true servant.

DESDEMONA: I know 't: I thank you: you do love my
 Lord:
 You have known him long, and be you well assur'd
 He shall in strangeness stand no farther off,
 Than in a politic distance.   5
CASSIO: Ay, but Lady,
 That policy may either last so long,
 Or feed upon such nice and waterish diet,
 Or breed itself so out of circumstances,
 That I being absent, and my place suppli'd,   10
 My General will forget my love, and service.
DESDEMONA: Do not doubt that: before Emilia here,
 I give thee warrant of thy place. Assure thee,
 If I do vow a friendship, I 'll perform it
 To the last article. My Lord shall never rest,   15
 I 'll watch him tame, and talk him out of patience;
 His bed shall seem a school, his board a shrift,
 I 'll intermingle every thing he does
 With Cassio's suit: therefore be merry Cassio,
 For thy solicitor shall rather die,   20
 Than give thy cause away.
                Enter Othello, and Iago.
EMILIA: Madam, here comes my Lord.
CASSIO: Madam, I 'll take my leave.
DESDEMONA: Why stay, and hear me speak.   25
CASSIO: Madam, not now: I am very ill at ease,
 Unfit for mine own purposes.
DESDEMONA: Well, do your discretion. *Exit Cassio.*
IAGO: Hah? I like not that.
OTHELLO: What dost thou say?   30
IAGO: Nothing my Lord; or if – I know not what.
OTHELLO: Was not that Cassio parted from my wife?
IAGO: Cassio my Lord? No sure, I cannot think it

That he would steal away so guilty-like,
Seeing your coming.

OTHELLO: I do believe 'twas he.

DESDEMONA: How now my Lord?

5   I have been talking with a suitor here,
A man that languishes in your displeasure.

OTHELLO: Who is 't you mean?

DESDEMONA: Why your Lieutenant Cassio: Good my Lord,

10   If I have any grace, or power to move you,
His present reconciliation take.
For if he be not one, that truly loves you,
That errs in ignorance, and not in cunning,
I have no judgement in an honest face.

15   I prithee call him back.

OTHELLO: Went he hence now?

DESDEMONA: Ay sooth; so humbled,
That he hath left part of his grief with me
To suffer with him. Good Love, call him back.

20 OTHELLO: Not now (sweet Desdemon) some other time.

DESDEMONA: But shall 't be shortly?

OTHELLO: The sooner (Sweet) for you.

DESDEMONA: Shall 't be tonight, at supper?

OTHELLO: No, not tonight.

25 DESDEMONA: Tomorrow dinner then?

OTHELLO: I shall not dine at home:
I meet the Captains at the Citadel.

DESDEMONA: Why then tomorrow night, on Tuesday morn,

30   On Tuesday noon, or night; on Wednesday morn.
I prithee name the time, but let it not
Exceed three days. In faith he's penitent:
And yet his trespass, in our common reason

(Save that they say the wars must make example)
Out of her best, is not almost a fault
T' incur a private check. When shall he come?
Tell me Othello. I wonder in my soul
What you would ask me, that I should deny,   5
Or stand so mamm'ring on? What? Michael Cassio,
That came a-wooing with you? and so many a time
(When I have spoke of you dispraisingly)
Hath ta'en your part, to have so much to do
To bring him in? Birlady, I could do much.   10

OTHELLO: Prithee no more: Let him come when he
    will:
    I will deny thee nothing.

DESDEMONA: Why, this is not a boon:
    'Tis as I should entreat you wear your gloves,   15
    Or feed on nourishing dishes, or keep you warm,
    Or sue to you, to do a peculiar profit
    To your own person. Nay, when I have a suit
    Wherein I mean to touch your love indeed,
    It shall be full of poise, and difficult weight,   20
    And fearful to be granted.

OTHELLO: I will deny thee nothing.
    Whereon, I do beseech thee, grant me this,
    To leave me but a little to myself.

DESDEMONA: Shall I deny you? No: farewell my Lord.   25

OTHELLO: Farewell my Desdemona, I 'll come to thee
    straight.

DESDEMONA: Emilia come; be as your fancies teach you:
    Whate'er you be, I am obedient.
        Exeunt Desdemona and Emilia.   30

OTHELLO: Excellent wretch: Perdition catch my soul
    But I do love thee: and when I love thee not,
    Chaos is come again.

IAGO: My noble Lord.

OTHELLO: What dost thou say, Iago?

IAGO: Did Michael Cassio
  When he woo'd my Lady, know of your love?

5 OTHELLO: He did, from first to last:
  Why dost thou ask?

IAGO: But for a satisfaction of my thought,
  No further harm.

OTHELLO: Why of thy thought, Iago?

10 IAGO: I did not think he had been acquainted with her.

OTHELLO: O yes, and went between us very oft.

IAGO: Indeed?

OTHELLO: Indeed? Ay indeed. Discern'st thou aught in
    that?

15   Is he not honest?

IAGO: Honest, my Lord?

OTHELLO: Honest? Ay honest.

IAGO: My Lord, for aught I know.

OTHELLO: What dost thou think?

20 IAGO: Think, my Lord?

OTHELLO: Think, my Lord? By Heaven, thou echo'st
    me;
  As if there were some Monster in thy thought
  Too hideous to be shown. Thou didst mean something:
25   I heard thee say even now, thou lik'st not that,
  When Cassio left my wife. What didst not like?
  And when I told thee, he was of my counsel,
  Of my whole course of wooing; thou criedst, Indeed?
  And didst contract, and purse thy brow together,
30   As if thou then hadst shut up in thy brain
  Some horrible conceit. If thou dost love me,
  Show me thy thought.

IAGO: My Lord, you know I love you.

OTHELLO: I think thou dost:
    And for I know thou 'rt full of love, and honesty,
    And weigh'st thy words before thou giv'st them
        breath,
    Therefore these stops of thine, fright me the more: 5
    For such things in a false disloyal knave
    Are tricks of custom: but in a man that 's just,
    They're close dilations, working from the heart,
    That passion cannot rule.

IAGO: For Michael Cassio,   10
    I dare be sworn, I think that he is honest.

OTHELLO: I think so too.

IAGO: Men should be what they seem,
    Or those that be not, would they might seem none.

OTHELLO: Certain, men should be what they seem.   15

IAGO: Why then I think Cassio 's an honest man.

OTHELLO: Nay, yet there 's more in this?
    I prithee speak to me, as to thy thinkings,
    As thou dost ruminate, and give thy worst of thoughts
    The worst of words.   20

IAGO: Good my Lord pardon me,
    Though I am bound to every act of duty,
    I am not bound to that: All slaves are free:
    Utter my thoughts? Why say, they are vile, and false?
    As where 's that Palace, whereinto foul things   25
    Sometimes intrude not? Who has that breast so pure,
    Wherein uncleanly apprehensions
    Keep leets, and law-days, and in sessions sit
    With meditations lawful?

OTHELLO: Thou dost conspire against thy friend (Iago)   30
    If thou but think'st him wrong'd, and mak'st his ear
    A stranger to thy thoughts.

IAGO: I do beseech you,

Though I perchance am vicious in my guess
(As I confess it is my nature's plague
To spy into abuses, and of my jealousy
Shapes faults that are not) that your wisdom
5   From one, that so imperfectly conceits,
Would take no notice, nor build yourself a trouble
Out of his scattering, and unsure observance:
It were not for your quiet, nor your good,
Nor for my manhood, honesty, and wisdom,
10   To let you know my thoughts.
OTHELLO: What dost thou mean?
IAGO: Good name in man, and woman (dear my Lord)
Is the immediate jewel of their souls;
Who steals my purse, steals trash:
15   'Tis something, nothing;
'Twas mine, 'tis his, and has been slave to thousands:
But he that filches from me my good name,
Robs me of that, which not enriches him,
And makes me poor indeed.
20   OTHELLO: By Heaven I 'll know thy thoughts.
IAGO: You cannot, if my heart were in your hand,
Nor shall not, whilst 'tis in my custody.
OTHELLO: Ha?
IAGO: Oh, beware my Lord, of jealousy,
25   It is the green-ey'd Monster, which doth mock
The meat it feeds on. That cuckold lives in bliss,
Who certain of his fate, loves not his wronger:
But oh, what damned minutes tells he o'er,
Who dotes, yet doubts: Suspects, yet soundly loves?
30   OTHELLO: O misery.
IAGO: Poor, and content, is rich, and rich enough,
But riches fineless, is as poor as Winter,
To him that ever fears he shall be poor:

Good God, the souls of all my tribe defend
From jealousy.
OTHELLO: Why? why is this?
Think'st thou, I 'ld make a life of jealousy;
To follow still the changes of the Moon   5
With fresh suspicions? No: to be once in doubt,
Is once to be resolv'd: Exchange me for a goat,
When I shall turn the business of my soul
To such exsufflicate, and blown surmises,
Matching thy inference. 'Tis not to make me jealous,   10
To say my wife is fair, feeds well, loves company,
Is free of speech, sings, plays, and dances:
Where virtue is, these are more virtuous.
Nor from mine own weak merits, will I draw
The smallest fear, or doubt of her revolt,   15
For she had eyes, and chose me. No Iago,
I 'll see before I doubt; when I doubt, prove;
And on the proof, there is no more but this,
Away at once with love, or jealousy.
IAGO: I am glad of this: For now I shall have reason   20
To show the love and duty that I bear you
With franker spirit. Therefore (as I am bound)
Receive it from me. I speak not yet of proof:
Look to your wife, observe her well with Cassio,
Wear your eyes, thus: not jealous, nor secure: 25
I would not have your free, and noble nature,
Out of self-bounty, be abus'd: Look to 't:
I know our country disposition well:
In Venice, they do let God see the pranks
They dare not show their husbands.   30
Their best conscience,
Is not to leave 't undone, but keep 't unknown.
OTHELLO: Dost thou say so?

IAGO: She did deceive her Father, marrying you,
And when she seem'd to shake, and fear your looks,
She lov'd them most.

OTHELLO: And so she did.

5   IAGO: Why go to then:
She that so young could give out such a seeming
To seel her Father's eyes up, close as oak,
He thought 'twas witchcraft.
But I am much to blame:
10   I humbly do beseech you of your pardon
For too much loving you.

OTHELLO: I am bound to thee for ever.

IAGO: I see this hath a little dash'd your spirits.

OTHELLO: Not a jot, not a jot.

15   IAGO: I' faith I fear it has:
I hope you will consider what is spoke
Comes from your love.
But I do see y' are mov'd:
I am to pray you, not to strain my speech
20   To grosser issues, nor to larger reach,
Than to suspicion.

OTHELLO: I will not.

IAGO: Should you do so (my Lord)
My speech should fall into such vile success,
25   Which my thoughts aim'd not.
Cassio 's my worthy friend:
My Lord, I see y' are mov'd.

OTHELLO: No, not much mov'd:
I do not think but Desdemona's honest.

30   IAGO: Long live she so;
And long live you to think so.

OTHELLO: And yet how Nature erring from itself.

IAGO: Ay, there 's the point:

As (to be bold with you)
Not to affect many proposed matches
Of her own clime, complexion, and degree,
Whereto we see in all things, Nature tends:
Foh, one may smell in such, a will most rank,   5
Foul disproportions, thoughts unnatural.
But (pardon me) I do not in position
Distinctly speak of her, though I may fear
Her will, recoiling to her better judgement,
May fall to match you with her country forms,   10
And happily repent.

OTHELLO: Farewell, farewell:
If more thou dost perceive, let me know more:
Set on thy wife to observe.
Leave me Iago.   15

IAGO: My Lord, I take my leave.

OTHELLO: Why did I marry?
This honest creature (doubtless)
Sees, and knows more, much more than he unfolds.

IAGO: My Lord, I would I might entreat your Honour   20
To scan this thing no farther: Leave it to time,
Although 'tis fit that Cassio have his place;
For sure he fills it up with great ability;
Yet if you please, to hold him off awhile:
You shall by that perceive him, and his means: 25
Note if your Lady strain his entertainment
With any strong, or vehement importunity,
Much will be seen in that: In the mean time,
Let me be thought too busy in my fears,
(As worthy cause I have to fear I am)   30
And hold her free, I do beseech your Honour.

OTHELLO: Fear not my government.

IAGO: I once more take my leave.   *Exit.*

OTHELLO: This fellow 's of exceeding honesty,
And knows all quantities with a learn'd spirit
Of human dealings. If I do prove her haggard,
Though that her jesses were my dear heart-strings,
5   I 'ld whistle her off, and let her down the wind
To prey at Fortune. Haply, for I am black,
And have not those soft parts of conversation
That chamberers have: Or for I am declin'd
Into the vale of years (yet that 's not much)
10   She 's gone. I am abus'd, and my relief
Must be to loathe her. Oh curse of marriage!
That we can call these delicate creatures ours,
And not their appetites! I had rather be a toad,
And live upon the vapour of a dungeon,
15   Than keep a corner in the thing I love
For others' uses. Yet 'tis the plague to Great-ones,
Prerogativ'd are they less than the base,
'Tis destiny unshunnable, like death:
Even then, this forked plague is fated to us,
20   When we do quicken. Look where she comes:
　　　　　Enter Desdemona and Emilia.
If she be false, Heaven mock'd itself:
I 'll not believe 't.
DESDEMONA: How now, my dear Othello?
25   Your dinner, and the generous Islanders
By you invited, do attend your presence.
OTHELLO: I am to blame.
DESDEMONA: Why do you speak so faintly?
Are you not well?
30   OTHELLO: I have a pain upon my forehead, here.
DESDEMONA: Faith that 's with watching, 'twill away again.
Let me but bind it hard, within this hour

It will be well.

OTHELLO: Your napkin is too little:
Let it alone: Come, I'll go in with you.

DESDEMONA: I am very sorry that you are not well.
Exeunt Othello and Desdemona.   5

EMILIA: I am glad I have found this napkin:
This was her first remembrance from the Moor,
My wayward husband hath a hundred times
Woo'd me to steal it. But she so loves the token,
(For he conjur'd her, she should ever keep it)   10
That she reserves it evermore about her,
To kiss, and talk to. I'll have the work ta'en out,
And give 't Iago: what he will do with it
Heaven knows, not I:
I nothing, but to please his fantasy.   15
Enter Iago.

IAGO: How now? What do you here alone?

EMILIA: Do not you chide: I have a thing for you.

IAGO: You have a thing for me?
It is a common thing –   20

EMILIA: Hah?

IAGO: To have a foolish wife.

EMILIA: Oh, is that all? What will you give me now
For that same handkerchief?

IAGO: What handkerchief?   25

EMILIA: What handkerchief?
Why that the Moor first gave to Desdemona,
That which so often you did bid me steal.

IAGO: Hast stolen it from her?

EMILIA: No faith, she let it drop by negligence,   30
And to th' advantage, I being here, took 't up:
Look, here 'tis.

IAGO: A good wench, give it me.

EMILIA: What will you do with 't, that you have been so
earnest to have me filch it?

IAGO: Why, what is that to you?

EMILIA: If it be not for some purpose of import,
5   Give 't me again. Poor Lady, she 'll run mad
When she shall lack it.

IAGO: Be not acknown on 't:
I have use for it. Go, leave me.   *Exit Emilia.*
I will in Cassio's lodging lose this napkin,
10   And let him find it. Trifles light as air,
Are to the jealous, confirmations strong,
As proofs of holy Writ. This may do something.
The Moor already changes with my poison:
Dangerous conceits, are in their natures poisons,
15   Which at the first are scarce found to distaste:
But with a little act upon the blood,
Burn like the mines of sulphur. I did say so.
              Enter Othello.
Look where he comes: Not poppy, nor mandragora,
20   Nor all the drowsy syrups of the world
Shall ever medicine thee to that sweet sleep
Which thou ow'dst yesterday.

OTHELLO: Ha, ha, false to me?

IAGO: Why how now General? No more of that.

25 OTHELLO: Avaunt, be gone: Thou has set me on the
rack:
I swear 'tis better to be much abus'd,
Than but to know 't a little.

IAGO: How now, my Lord?

30 OTHELLO: What sense had I, in her stol'n hours of lust?
I saw 't not, thought it not: it harm'd not me:
I slept the next night well, fed well, was free, and merry.
I found not Cassio's kisses on her lips:

He that is robb'd, not wanting what is stol'n,
Let him not know 't, and he 's not robb'd at all.
IAGO: I am sorry to hear this!
OTHELLO: I had been happy, if the general camp,
Pioners and all, had tasted her sweet body,   5
So I had nothing known. Oh now, for ever
Farewell the tranquil mind; farewell content;
Farewell the plumed troops, and the big wars,
That makes ambition, virtue! Oh farewell,
Farewell the neighing steed, and the shrill trump,   10
The spirit-stirring drum, th' ear-piercing fife,
The royal banner, and all quality,
Pride, pomp, and circumstance of glorious War:
And O you mortal engines, whose rude throats
Th' immortal Jove's dread clamours, counterfeit,   15
Farewell: Othello's occupation 's gone.
IAGO: Is 't possible my Lord?
OTHELLO: Villain, be sure thou prove my Love a whore;
Be sure of it: Give me the ocular proof,
Or by the worth of mine eternal soul,   20
Thou hadst been better have been born a dog
Than answer my wak'd wrath.
IAGO: Is 't come to this?
OTHELLO: Make me to see't: or (at the least) so prove it,
That the probation bear no hinge, nor loop,   25
To hang a doubt on: Or woe upon thy life.
IAGO: My noble Lord.
OTHELLO: If thou dost slander her, and torture me,
Never pray more: Abandon all remorse;
On horror's head, horrors accumulate: 30
Do deeds to make Heaven weep, all Earth amaz'd;
For nothing canst thou to damnation add,
Greater than that.

IAGO: O Grace! O Heaven forgive me!
Are you a man? Have you a soul? or sense?
God buy you: take mine office. Oh wretched fool,
That lov'st to make thine honesty, a vice!
5   Oh monstrous world! Take note, take note (O World)
To be direct and honest, is not safe.
I thank you for this profit, and from hence
I'll love no friend, sith love breeds such offence.
OTHELLO: Nay stay: thou shouldst be honest.
10 IAGO: I should be wise; for honesty 's a fool,
And loses that it works for.
OTHELLO: By the World,
I think my wife be honest, and think she is not:
I think that thou art just, and think thou art not:
15   I 'll have some proof. My name that was as fresh
As Dian's visage, is now begrim'd and black
As mine own face. If there be cords, or knives,
Poison, or fire, or suffocating streams,
I 'll not endure it. Would I were satisfied.
20 IAGO: I see you are eaten up with passion:
I do repent me, that I put it to you.
You would be satisfied?
OTHELLO: Would? Nay, and I will.
IAGO: And may: but how? How satisfied, my Lord?
25   Would you the supervision grossly gape on?
Behold her topp'd?
OTHELLO: Death, and damnation. Oh!
IAGO: It were a tedious difficulty, I think,
To bring them to that prospect: Damn them then,
30   If ever mortal eyes do see them bolster
More than their own. What then? How then?
What shall I say? Where 's satisfaction?
It is impossible you should see this,

Were they as prime as goats, as hot as monkeys,
As salt as wolves in pride, and fools as gross
As ignorance, made drunk. But yet, I say,
If imputation, and strong circumstances,
Which lead directly to the door of Truth,   5
Will give you satisfaction, you might have 't.

OTHELLO: Give me a living reason she's disloyal.

IAGO: I do not like the office.
But sith I am enter'd in this cause so far
(Prick'd to 't by foolish honesty, and love)   10
I will go on. I lay with Cassio lately,
And being troubled with a raging tooth,
I could not sleep. There are a kind of men,
So loose of soul, that in their sleeps will mutter
Their affairs: one of this kind is Cassio: 15
In sleep I heard him say, sweet Desdemona,
Let us be wary, let us hide our loves,
And then (Sir) would he gripe, and wring my hand:
Cry, oh sweet creature: then kiss me hard,
As if he pluck'd up kisses by the roots,   20
That grew upon my lips, laid his leg over my thigh,
And sigh, and kiss, and then cry cursed Fate,
That gave thee to the Moor.

OTHELLO: O monstrous! monstrous!

IAGO: Nay, this was but his dream.   25

OTHELLO: But this denoted a foregone conclusion,
'Tis a shrewd doubt, though it be but a dream.

IAGO: And this may help to thicken other proofs,
That do demonstrate thinly.

OTHELLO: I 'll tear her all to pieces.   30

IAGO: Nay yet be wise; yet we see nothing done,
She may be honest yet: Tell me but this,
Have you not sometimes seen a handkerchief

    Spotted with strawberries, in your wife's hand?

OTHELLO: I gave her such a one: 'twas my first gift.

IAGO: I know not that: but such a handkerchief
    (I am sure it was your wife's) did I today
5   See Cassio wipe his beard with.

OTHELLO: If it be that.

IAGO: If it be that, or any, it was hers,
    It speaks against her with the other proofs.

OTHELLO: O that the slave had forty thousand lives:
10   One is too poor, too weak for my revenge.
    Now do I see 'tis true. Look here Iago,
    All my fond love thus do I blow to Heaven. 'Tis gone.
    Arise black vengeance, from the hollow hell,
    Yield up (O Love) thy crown, and hearted throne
15   To tyrannous hate. Swell bosom with thy fraught,
    For 'tis of aspics' tongues.

IAGO: Yet be content.

OTHELLO: Oh blood, blood, blood.

IAGO: Patience I say: your mind may change.

20 OTHELLO: Never Iago. Like to the Pontic Sea,
    Whose icy current, and compulsive course,
    Ne'er keeps retiring ebb, but keeps due on
    To the Propontic, and the Hellespont:
    Even so my bloody thoughts, with violent pace
25   Shall ne'er look back, ne'er ebb to humble love
    Till that a capable, and wide revenge
    Swallow them up. Now by yond marble Heaven,
    In the due reverence of a sacred vow,
    I here engage my words.

30 IAGO: Do not rise yet:
    Witness you ever-burning lights above,
    You elements, that clip us round about,   *Iago kneels.*
    Witness that here Iago doth give up

    The execution of his wit, hands, heart,
    To wrong'd Othello's service. Let him command,
    And to obey shall be in me remorse,
    What bloody business ever.

OTHELLO: I greet thy love,   5
    Not with vain thanks, but with acceptance bounteous,
    And will upon the instant put thee to 't.
    Within these three days let me hear thee say,
    That Cassio 's not alive.

IAGO: My friend is dead: 10
    'Tis done at your request.
    But let her live.

OTHELLO: Damn her lewd minx:
    O damn her, damn her.
    Come go with me apart, I will withdraw   15
    To furnish me with some swift means of death
    For the fair Devil.
    Now art thou my Lieutenant.

IAGO: I am your own for ever.
                    Exeunt.   20

III.4

Enter Desdemona, Emilia, and Clown.

DESDEMONA: Do you know Sirrah, where Lieutenant
    Cassio lies?

CLOWN: I dare not say he lies any where.   25

DESDEMONA: Why man?

CLOWN: He 's a soldier, and for me to say a soldier lies,
    'tis stabbing.

DESDEMONA: Go to: where lodges he?

CLOWN: To tell you where he lodges, is to tell you where 30
    I lie.

DESDEMONA: Can any thing be made of this?

CLOWN: I know not where he lodges, and for me to devise a lodging, and say he lies here, or he lies there, were to lie in mine own throat.

5 DESDEMONA: Can you inquire him out? and be edified by report?

CLOWN: I will catechize the world for him, that is, make questions, and by them answer.

DESDEMONA: Seek him, bid him come hither: tell him, 10 I have mov'd my Lord on his behalf, and hope all will be well.

CLOWN: To do this, is within the compass of man's wit, and therefore I will attempt the doing it.

Exit Clown.

15 DESDEMONA: Where should I lose the handkerchief, Emilia?

EMILIA: I know not Madam.

DESDEMONA: Believe me, I had rather have lost my purse Full of crusadoes. And but my noble Moor
20 Is true of mind, and made of no such baseness,
As jealous creatures are, it were enough
To put him to ill thinking.

EMILIA: Is he not jealous?

DESDEMONA: Who, he? I think the Sun where he was
25 born,
Drew all such humours from him.

EMILIA: Look where he comes.

Enter Othello.

DESDEMONA: I will not leave him now, till Cassio
30 Be call'd to him. How is 't with you, my Lord?

OTHELLO: Well my good Lady. Oh hardness to dissemble!
How do you, Desdemona?

DESDEMONA: Well, my good Lord.

OTHELLO: Give me your hand.
This hand is moist my Lady.

DESDEMONA: It hath felt no age, nor known no sorrow.

OTHELLO: This argues fruitfulness, and liberal heart: 5
Hot, hot, and moist. This hand of yours requires
A sequester from liberty: fasting, and prayer,
Much castigation, exercise devout,
For here's a young, and sweating devil here
That commonly rebels: 'Tis a good hand,   10
A frank one.

DESDEMONA: You may (indeed) say so:
For 'twas that hand that gave away my heart.

OTHELLO: A liberal hand. The hearts of old, gave hands:
But our new heraldry is hands, not hearts.   15

DESDEMONA: I cannot speak of this:
Come, now your promise.

OTHELLO: What promise, Chuck?

DESDEMONA: I have sent to bid Cassio come speak with
you.   20

OTHELLO: I have a salt and sorry rheum offends me:
Lend me thy handkerchief.

DESDEMONA: Here my Lord.

OTHELLO: That which I gave you.

DESDEMONA: I have it not about me.   25

OTHELLO: Not?

DESDEMONA: No indeed, my Lord.

OTHELLO: That's a fault: That handkerchief
Did an Egyptian to my Mother give:
She was a charmer, and could almost read   30
The thoughts of people. She told her, while she kept it,
'Twould make her amiable, and subdue my father
Entirely to her love: But if she lost it,

Or made a gift of it, my Father's eye
Should hold her loathed, and his spirits should hunt
After new fancies. She dying, gave it me,
And bid me (when my Fate would have me wiv'd),
5   To give it her. I did so; and take heed on 't,
Make it a darling, like your precious eye:
To lose 't, or give 't away, were such perdition,
As nothing else could match.

DESDEMONA: Is 't possible?

10   OTHELLO: 'Tis true: There 's magic in the web of it:
A Sibyl that had number'd in the world
The Sun to course, two hundred compasses,
In her prophetic fury sew'd the work:
The worms were hallow'd, that did breed the silk,
15   And it was dyed in mummy, which the skilful
Conserv'd of maidens' hearts.

DESDEMONA: Indeed? Is 't true?

OTHELLO: Most veritable, therefore look to 't well.

DESDEMONA: Then would to God, that I had never
20   seen 't!

OTHELLO: Ha? wherefore?

DESDEMONA: Why do you speak so startingly, and rash?

OTHELLO: Is 't lost? Is 't gone? Speak, is it out o' th' way?

DESDEMONA: Bless us.

25   OTHELLO: Say you?

DESDEMONA: It is not lost: but what and if it were?

OTHELLO: How?

DESDEMONA: I say it is not lost.

OTHELLO: Fetch 't, let me see 't.

30   DESDEMONA: Why so I can: but I will not now:
This is a trick to put me from my suit,
Pray you let Cassio be receiv'd again.

OTHELLO: Fetch me the handkerchief,

My mind misgives.

DESDEMONA: Come, come: You 'll never meet a more
sufficient man.

OTHELLO: The handkerchief.

DESDEMONA: A man that all his time   5
Hath founded his good fortunes on your love;
Shar'd dangers with you.

OTHELLO: The handkerchief.

DESDEMONA: In sooth you are to blame.

OTHELLO: Zounds.   10

Exit Othello.

EMILIA: Is not this man jealous?

DESDEMONA: I ne'er saw this before.
Sure, there 's some wonder in this handkerchief,
I am most unhappy in the loss of it.   15

EMILIA: 'Tis not a year or two shows us a man:
They are all but stomachs, and we all but food,
They eat us hungerly, and when they are full
They belch us.

Enter Iago and Cassio.   20

Look you, Cassio and my husband.

IAGO: There is no other way: 'tis she must do 't:
And lo the happiness: go, and importune her.

DESDEMONA: How now (good Cassio) what 's the news
with you?   25

CASSIO: Madam, my former suit. I do beseech you,
That by your virtuous means, I may again
Exist, and be a member of his love,
Whom I, with all the office of my heart
Entirely honour, I would not be delay'd.   30
If my offence, be of such mortal kind,
That nor my service past, nor present sorrows,
Nor purpos'd merit in futurity,

Can ransom me into his love again,
But to know so, must be my benefit:
So shall I clothe me in a forc'd content,
And shut myself up in some other course
5 To Fortune's alms.

DESDEMONA: Alas (thrice-gentle Cassio)
My advocation is not now in tune;
My Lord, is not my Lord; nor should I know him,
Were he in favour, as in humour alter'd.
10 So help me every spirit sanctified,
As I have spoken for you all my best,
And stood within the blank of his displeasure
For my free speech. You must awhile be patient:
What I can do, I will: and more I will
15 Than for myself, I dare. Let that suffice you.

IAGO: Is my Lord angry?

EMILIA: He went hence but now:
And certainly in strange unquietness.

IAGO: Can he be angry? I have seen the cannon
20 When it hath blown his ranks into the air,
And like the Devil from his very arm
Puff'd his own brother: And he is angry?
Something of moment then: I will go meet him,
There 's matter in 't indeed, if he be angry.   *Exit.*

25 DESDEMONA: I prithee do so. Something sure of state,
Either from Venice, or some unhatch'd practice
Made demonstrable here in Cyprus, to him,
Hath puddled his clear spirit: and in such cases,
Men's natures wrangle with inferior things,
30 Though great ones are their object. 'Tis even so.
For let our finger ache, and it indues
Our other healthful members, even to a sense
Of pain. Nay, we must think men are not Gods,

Nor of them look for such observancy
As fits the bridal. Beshrew me much, Emilia,
I was (unhandsome warrior, as I am)
Arraigning his unkindness with my soul:
But now I find, I had suborn'd the witness,   5
And he 's indicted falsely.

EMILIA: Pray heaven it be
State matters, as you think, and no conception,
Nor no jealous toy, concerning you.

DESDEMONA: Alas the day, I never gave him cause.   10

EMILIA: But jealous souls will not be answer'd so;
They are not ever jealous for the cause,
But jealous, for they 're jealous. It is a Monster
Begot upon itself, born on itself.

DESDEMONA: Heaven keep the Monster from Othello's   15
mind.

EMILIA: Lady, Amen.

DESDEMONA: I will go seek him. Cassio, walk here about:
If I do find him fit, I 'll move your suit,
And seek to effect it to my uttermost.   20

Exeunt Desdemona and Emilia.

CASSIO: I humbly thank your Ladyship.

Enter Bianca.

BIANCA: 'Save you (friend Cassio).

CASSIO: What make you from home?   25
How is 't with you, my most fair Bianca?
Indeed (sweet Love) I was coming to your house.

BIANCA: And I was going to your lodging, Cassio.
What? keep a week away? Seven days, and nights?
Eight score eight hours? And lovers' absent hours   30
More tedious than the dial, eight score times?
Oh weary reckoning.

CASSIO: Pardon me, Bianca:

I have this while with leaden thoughts been press'd,
But I shall in a more continuate time
Strike off this score of absence. Sweet Bianca
Take me this work out.

5 BIANCA: Oh Cassio, whence came this?
This is some token from a newer friend,
To the felt absence: now I feel a cause:
Is 't come to this? Well, well.

CASSIO: Go to, woman:

10 . Throw your vile guesses in the Devil's teeth,
From whence you have them. You are jealous now,
That this is from some Mistress, some remembrance;
No, in good troth Bianca.

BIANCA: Why, whose is it?

15 CASSIO: I know not neither:
I found it in my chamber,
I like the work well; Ere it be demanded
(As like enough it will) I would have it copied:
Take it, and do 't, and leave me for this time.

20 BIANCA: Leave you? Wherefore?

CASSIO: I do attend here on the General,
And think it no addition, nor my wish
To have him see me woman'd.

BIANCA: Why, I pray you?

25 CASSIO: Not that I love you not.

BIANCA: But that you do not love me.
I pray you bring me on the way a little,
And say, if I shall see you soon at night?

CASSIO: 'Tis but a little way that I can bring you,

30 For I attend here: But I 'll see you soon.

BIANCA: 'Tis very good: I must be circumstanc'd.
Exeunt.

Enter Othello, and Iago.

IAGO: Will you think so?

OTHELLO: Think so, Iago?

IAGO: What, to kiss in private?   5

OTHELLO: An unauthoriz'd kiss?

IAGO: Or to be naked with her friend in bed,
    An hour, or more, not meaning any harm?

OTHELLO: Naked in bed (Iago) and not mean harm?
    It is hypocrisy against the Devil: 10
    They that mean virtuously, and yet do so,
    The Devil their virtue tempts, and they tempt Heaven.

IAGO: If they do nothing, 'tis a venial slip:
    But if I give my wife a handkerchief.

OTHELLO: What then?   15

IAGO: Why then 'tis hers (my Lord) and being hers,
    She may (I think) bestow 't on any man.

OTHELLO: She is protectress of her honour too:
    May she give that?

IAGO: Her honour is an essence that 's not seen,   20
    They have it very oft, that have it not.
    But for the handkerchief.

OTHELLO: By heaven, I would most gladly have forgot it:
    Thou said'st (oh, it comes o'er my memory,
    As doth the raven o'er the infectious house: 25
    Boding to all) he had my handkerchief.

IAGO: Ay: what of that?

OTHELLO: That 's not so good now.

IAGO: What if I had said, I had seen him do you wrong?
    Or heard him say (as knaves be such abroad,   30
    Who having by their own importunate suit,

Or voluntary dotage of some Mistress,
Convinced or suppli'd them, cannot choose
But they must blab.)

OTHELLO: Hath he said anything?

5 IAGO: He hath (my Lord) but be you well assur'd,
No more than he 'll unswear.

OTHELLO: What hath he said?

IAGO: Faith, that he did: I know not what he did.

OTHELLO: What? What?

10 IAGO: Lie.

OTHELLO: With her?

IAGO: With her? On her: what you will.

OTHELLO: Lie with her? lie on her? We say lie on her,
when they be-lie-her. Lie with her: 'zounds, that 's
15 fulsome: Handkerchief: Confessions: Handkerchief. To
confess, and be hang'd for his labour. First, to be hang'd,
and then to confess: I tremble at it. Nature would not
invest herself in such shadowing passion, without some
instruction. It is not words that shakes me thus, (pish)
20 noses, ears, and lips: is 't possible. Confess? Handkerchief? O devil.   *Falls in a trance.*

IAGO: Work on,
My medicine works. Thus credulous fools are caught,
And many worthy, and chaste dames even thus,
25 (All guiltless) meet reproach: what hoa? My Lord?
My Lord, I say: Othello.

Enter Cassio.

How now Cassio?

CASSIO: What 's the matter?

30 IAGO: My Lord is fall'n into an epilepsy,
This is his second fit: he had one yesterday.

CASSIO: Rub him about the temples.

IAGO: No forbear,

The lethargy must have his quiet course:
If not, he foams at mouth: and by and by
Breaks out to savage madness. Look, he stirs:
Do you withdraw yourself a little while,
He will recover straight: when he is gone,   5
I would on great occasion, speak with you.

Exit Cassio.

How is it General? Have you not hurt your head?

OTHELLO: Dost thou mock me?

IAGO: I mock you not, by Heaven: 10
Would you would bear your fortune like a man.

OTHELLO: A horned man's a monster, and a beast.

IAGO: There's many a beast then in a populous city,
And many a civil monster.

OTHELLO: Did he confess it?   15

IAGO: Good sir, be a man:
Think every bearded fellow that's but yok'd
May draw with you. There's millions now alive,
That nightly lie in those unproper beds,
Which they dare swear peculiar. Your case is better.   20
Oh, 'tis the spite of hell, the Fiend's arch-mock,
To lip a wanton in a secure couch;
And to suppose her chaste. No, let me know,
And knowing what I am, I know what she shall be.

OTHELLO: Oh, thou art wise: 'tis certain.   25

IAGO: Stand you awhile apart,
Confine yourself but in a patient list,
Whilst you were here, o'erwhelmed with your grief
(A passion most unsuiting such a man)
Cassio came hither. I shifted him away,   30
And laid good 'scuses upon your ecstasy,
Bad him anon return: and here speak with me,
The which he promis'd. Do but encave yourself,

And mark the fleers, the gibes, and notable scorns
That dwell in every region of his face;
For I will make him tell the tale anew;
Where, how, how oft, how long ago, and when
5   He hath, and is again to cope your wife.
I say, but mark his gesture: marry patience,
Or I shall say y' are all in all in spleen,
And nothing of a man.
OTHELLO: Dost thou hear, Iago,
10   I will be found most cunning in my patience:
But (dost thou hear) most bloody.
IAGO: That 's not amiss,
But yet keep time in all: will you withdraw?
[Othello hides himself.]
15   Now will I question Cassio of Bianca,
A housewife that by selling her desires
Buys herself bread, and cloth. It is a creature
That dotes on Cassio, (as 'tis the strumpet's plague
To beguile many, and be beguil'd by one)
20   He, when he hears of her, cannot restrain
From the excess of laughter. Here he comes.
Enter Cassio.
As he shall smile, Othello shall go mad:
And his unbookish jealousy must conserve
25   Poor Cassio's smiles, gestures, and light behaviours
Quite in the wrong. How do you Lieutenant?
CASSIO: The worser, than you give me the addition,
Whose want even kills me.
IAGO: Ply Desdemona well, and you are sure on 't:
30   Now, if this suit lay in Bianca's dower,
How quickly should you speed?
CASSIO: Alas poor caitiff.
OTHELLO: Look how he laughs already.

IAGO: I never knew woman love man so.

CASSIO: Alas poor rogue, I think i' faith she loves me.

OTHELLO: Now he denies it faintly: and laughs it out.

IAGO: Do you hear Cassio?

OTHELLO: Now he importunes him   5
    To tell it o'er: go to, well said, well said.

IAGO: She gives it out, that you shall marry her.
    Do you intend it?

CASSIO: Ha, ha, ha.

OTHELLO: Do ye triumph, Roman? do you triumph?   10

CASSIO: I marry. What? A customer; prithee bear
    Some charity to my wit, do not think it
    So unwholesome. Ha, ha, ha.

OTHELLO: So, so, so, so: they laugh, that wins.

IAGO: Faith the cry goes, that you marry her.   15

CASSIO: Prithee say true.

IAGO: I am a very villain else.

OTHELLO: Have you scor'd me? Well.

CASSIO: This is the monkey's own giving out:
    She is persuaded I will marry her   20
    Out of her own love and flattery, not out of my promise.

OTHELLO: Iago beckons me: now he begins the story.

CASSIO: She was here even now: she haunts me in every
    place. I was the other day talking on the sea-bank
    with certain Venetians, and thither comes the bauble, 25
    by this hand she falls me thus about my neck.

OTHELLO: Crying oh dear Cassio, as it were: his gesture
    imports it.

CASSIO: So hangs, and lolls, and weeps upon me:
    So shakes, and pulls me. Ha, ha, ha.   30

OTHELLO: Now he tells how she pluck'd him to my
    chamber: oh, I see that nose of yours, but not that dog,
    I shall throw it to.

CASSIO: Well, I must leave her company.

IAGO: Before me: look where she comes.

Enter Bianca.

CASSIO: 'Tis such another fitchew: marry a perfum'd
5   one?

What do you mean by this haunting of me?

BIANCA: Let the devil, and his dam haunt you: what did
you mean by that same handkerchief, you gave me
even now? I was a fine fool to take it: I must take out
10   the work? A likely piece of work, that you should find
it in your chamber, and know not who left it there.
This is some minx's token, and I must take out the work?
There, give it your hobbyhorse, wheresoever you had it, ·
I'll take out no work on't.

15 CASSIO: How now, my sweet Bianca?
How now? How now?

OTHELLO: By Heaven, that should be my handkerchief.

BIANCA: If you'll come to supper tonight you may, if
you will not, come when you are next prepar'd for. *Exit.*

20 IAGO: After her: after her.

CASSIO: Faith I must, she'll rail in the streets else.

IAGO: Will you sup there?

CASSIO: Faith I intend so.

IAGO: Well, I may chance to see you: for I would very
25   fain speak with you.

CASSIO: Prithee come: will you?

IAGO: Go to, say no more.   *Exit Cassio.*

OTHELLO: How shall I murther him, Iago.

IAGO: Did you perceive how he laugh'd at his vice?

30 OTHELLO: Oh, Iago.

IAGO: And did you see the handkerchief?

OTHELLO: Was that mine?

IAGO: Yours by this hand: and to see how he prizes

the foolish woman your wife: she gave it him, and he hath given it his whore.

OTHELLO: I would have him nine years a killing:
A fine woman, a fair woman, a sweet woman!

IAGO: Nay, you must forget that.   5

OTHELLO: Ay, let her rot and perish, and be damn'd to-night, for she shall not live. No, my heart is turn'd to stone: I strike it, and it hurts my hand. Oh, the world hath not a sweeter creature: she might lie by an Emperor's side, and command him tasks.   10

IAGO: Nay, that 's not your way.

OTHELLO: Hang her, I do but say what she is: so delicate with her needle: an admirable musician. Oh she will sing the savageness out of a bear: of so high and plenteous wit, and invention!   15

IAGO: She 's the worse for all this.

OTHELLO: Oh, a thousand, a thousand times:
And then be of so gentle a condition!

IAGO: Ay too gentle.

OTHELLO: Nay that 's certain: 20
But yet the pity of it, Iago: oh Iago, the pity of it Iago.

IAGO: If you are so fond over her iniquity: give her patent to offend, for if it touch not you, it comes near nobody.

OTHELLO: I will chop her into messes: cuckold me?   25

IAGO: Oh, 'tis foul in her.

OTHELLO: With mine Officer?

IAGO: That 's fouler.

OTHELLO: Get me some poison, Iago, this night. I 'll not expostulate with her: lest her body and beauty   30
unprovide my mind again: this night Iago.

IAGO: Do it not with poison, strangle her in her bed,
Even the bed she hath contaminated.

OTHELLO: Good, good:
The justice of it pleases: very good.
IAGO: And for Cassio, let me be his undertaker:
You shall hear more by midnight.

5   *A trumpet.*
Enter Lodovico, Desdemona, and Attendants.

OTHELLO: Excellent good: What trumpet is that same?
IAGO: I warrant something from Venice,
'Tis Lodovico, this comes from the Duke.
10   See, your wife 's with him.
LODOVICO: God save you worthy General.
OTHELLO: With all my heart Sir.
LODOVICO: The Duke, and the Senators of Venice greet
you.
15 OTHELLO: I kiss the instrument of their pleasures.
DESDEMONA: And what 's the news, good cousin Lodo-
vico?
IAGO: I am very glad to see you Signior:
Welcome to Cyprus.
20 LODOVICO: I thank you: how does Lieutenant Cassio?
IAGO: Lives Sir.
DESDEMONA: Cousin, there 's fall'n between him, and
my Lord,
An unkind breach: but you shall make all well.
25 OTHELLO: Are you sure of that?
DESDEMONA: My Lord?
OTHELLO: This fail you not to do, as you will —
LODOVICO: He did not call: he 's busy in the paper,
Is there division 'twixt my Lord, and Cassio?
30 DESDEMONA: A most unhappy one: I would do much
T' atone them, for the love I bear to Cassio.
OTHELLO: Fire, and brimstone.
DESDEMONA: My Lord.

OTHELLO: Are you wise?

DESDEMONA: What is he angry?

LODOVICO: May be th' letter mov'd him,
For as I think, they do command him home,
Deputing Cassio in his government.   5

DESDEMONA: By my troth, I am glad on 't.

OTHELLO: Indeed?

DESDEMONA: My Lord?

OTHELLO: I am glad to see you mad.

DESDEMONA: Why, sweet Othello?   10

OTHELLO: Devil.

DESDEMONA: I have not deserv'd this.

LODOVICO: My Lord, this would not be believ'd in
    Venice,
Though I should swear I saw 't. 'Tis very much,   15
Make her amends: she weeps.

OTHELLO: Oh devil, devil:
If that the Earth could teem with women's tears,
Each drop she falls, would prove a crocodile:
Out of my sight.   20

DESDEMONA: I will not stay to offend you.

LODOVICO: Truly obedient Lady:
I do beseech your Lordship call her back.

OTHELLO: Mistress.

DESDEMONA: My Lord.   25

OTHELLO: What would you with her, Sir?

LODOVICO: Who I, my Lord?

OTHELLO: Ay, you did wish, that I would make her turn:
Sir, she can turn, and turn: and yet go on
And turn again. And she can weep, Sir, weep.   30
And she 's obedient: as you say obedient.
Very obedient: proceed you in your tears.
Concerning this Sir, (oh well-painted passion)

I am commanded home: get you away:
I 'll send for you anon. Sir, I obey the mandate,
And will return to Venice. Hence, avaunt:
                    Exit Desdemona.
5   Cassio shall have my place. And Sir, tonight
I do entreat, that we may sup together.
You are welcome Sir, to Cyprus.
Goats, and monkeys.   *Exit.*
LODOVICO: Is this the noble Moor, whom our full Senate
10   Call all in all sufficient? Is this the nature
Whom passion could not shake? Whose solid virtue
The shot of accident, nor dart of chance
Could neither graze, nor pierce?
IAGO: He is much chang'd.
15   LODOVICO: Are his wits safe? Is he not light of brain?
IAGO: He 's that he is: I may not breathe my censure.
What he might be: if what he might, he is not,
I would to heaven he were.
LODOVICO: What? Strike his wife?
20   IAGO: 'Faith that was not so well: yet would I knew
That stroke would prove the worst.
LODOVICO: Is it his use?
Or did the letters, work upon his blood,
And new create his fault?
25   IAGO: Alas, alas:
It is not honesty in me to speak
What I have seen, and known. You shall observe him,
And his own courses will denote him so,
That I may save my speech: do but go after
30   And mark how he continues.
LODOVICO: I am sorry that I am deceiv'd in him.
                    Exeunt.

IV.2

Enter Othello, and Emilia.

OTHELLO: You have seen nothing then?

EMILIA: Nor ever heard: nor ever did suspect.

OTHELLO: Yes, you have seen Cassio, and she together.   5

EMILIA: But then I saw no harm: and then I heard,
Each syllable that breath made up between them.

OTHELLO: What? Did they never whisper?

EMILIA: Never my Lord.

OTHELLO: Nor send you out o' th' way?   10

EMILIA: Never.

OTHELLO: To fetch her fan, her gloves, her mask, nor
nothing?

EMILIA: Never my Lord.

OTHELLO: That 's strange.   15

EMILIA: I durst (my Lord) to wager, she is honest:
Lay down my soul at stake: If you think other,
Remove your thought. It doth abuse your bosom:
If any wretch have put this in your head,
Let Heaven requite it with the Serpent's curse,   20
For if she be not honest, chaste, and true,
There 's no man happy. The purest of their wives
Is foul as slander.

OTHELLO: Bid her come hither: go.   *Exit Emilia.*
She says enough: yet she 's a simple bawd   25
That cannot say as much. This is a subtle whore:
A closet lock and key of villainous secrets,
And yet she 'll kneel, and pray: I have seen her do 't.
Enter Desdemona, and Emilia.

DESDEMONA: My Lord, what is your will?   30

OTHELLO: Pray you Chuck come hither.

DESDEMONA: What is your pleasure?

OTHELLO: Let me see your eyes: look in my face.

DESDEMONA: What horrible fancy's this?

5 OTHELLO: Some of your function Mistress:
Leave procreants alone, and shut the door:
Cough, or cry hem; if any body come:
Your mystery, your mystery: nay dispatch.

Exit Emilia.

10 DESDEMONA: Upon my knee, what doth your speech
import?
I understand a fury in your words,
But not the words.

OTHELLO: Why? What art thou?

15 DESDEMONA: Your wife my Lord: your true and loyal
wife.

OTHELLO: Come swear it: damn thyself, lest being like
one of Heaven, the devils themselves should fear to
seize thee. Therefore be double-damn'd: swear thou art

20 honest.

DESDEMONA: Heaven doth truly know it.

OTHELLO: Heaven truly knows, that thou art false as hell.

DESDEMONA: To whom my Lord?
With whom? How am I false?

25 OTHELLO: Ah Desdemon, away, away, away.

DESDEMONA: Alas the heavy day: why do you weep?
Am I the motive of these tears my Lord?
If happily you my Father do suspect,
An instrument of this your calling back,

30 Lay not your blame on me: if you have lost him,
I have lost him too.

OTHELLO: Had it pleas'd Heaven,
To try me with affliction, had they rain'd

All kinds of sores, and shames on my bare head:
Steep'd me in poverty to the very lips,
Given to captivity, me, and my utmost hopes,
I should have found in some place of my soul
A drop of patience. But alas, to make me   5
The fixed figure for the time of Scorn,
To point his slow, and moving finger at.
Yet could I bear that too, well, very well:
But there where I have garner'd up my heart,
Where either I must live, or bear no life,   10
The fountain from the which my current runs,
Or else dries up: to be discarded thence,
Or keep it as a cistern, for foul toads
To knot and gender in. Turn thy complexion there:
Patience, thou young and rose-lipp'd cherubin,   15
I here look grim as hell.
DESDEMONA: I hope my noble Lord esteems me honest.
OTHELLO: Oh ay, as summer flies are in the shambles,
  That quicken even with blowing. Oh thou weed:
  Who art so lovely fair, and smell'st so sweet,   20
  That the sense aches at thee,
  Would thou hadst never been born.
DESDEMONA: Alas, what ignorant sin have I committed?
OTHELLO: Was this fair paper? This most goodly book
  Made to write whore upon? What committed,   25
  Committed? Oh, thou public commoner,
  I should make very forges of my cheeks,
  That would to cinders burn up modesty,
  Did I but speak thy deeds. What committed?
  Heaven stops the nose at it, and the Moon winks: 30
  The bawdy wind that kisses all it meets,
  Is hush'd within the hollow mine of Earth
  And will not hear 't. What committed?

Impudent strumpet!

DESDEMONA: By Heaven you do me wrong.

OTHELLO: Are not you a strumpet?

DESDEMONA: No, as I am a Christian.

5   If to preserve this vessel for my Lord,
     From any other foul unlawful touch
     Be not to be a strumpet, I am none.

OTHELLO: What, not a whore?

DESDEMONA: No, as I shall be sav'd.

10 OTHELLO: Is 't possible?

DESDEMONA: Oh Heaven forgive us.

OTHELLO: I cry you mercy then.
     I took you for that cunning whore of Venice,
     That married with Othello. You Mistress,

15   *Enter Emilia.*
     That have the office opposite to Saint Peter,
     And keeps the gate of hell. You, you: ay you.
     We have done our course: there 's money for your
     pains:

20   I pray you turn the key, and keep our counsel.   *Exit.*

EMILIA: Alas, what does this Gentleman conceive?
     How do you Madam? how do you my good Lady?

DESDEMONA: Faith, half asleep.

EMILIA: Good Madam,

25   What 's the matter with my Lord?

DESDEMONA: With who?

EMILIA: Why, with my Lord, Madam.

DESDEMONA: Who is thy Lord?

EMILIA: He that is yours, sweet Lady.

30 DESDEMONA: I have none: do not talk to me, Emilia,
     I cannot weep: nor answers I have none,
     But what should go by water. Prithee tonight,
     Lay on my bed my wedding sheets, remember,

And call thy husband hither.

EMILIA: Here's a change indeed.   *Exit.*

DESDEMONA: 'Tis meet I should be us'd so: very meet.
How have I been behav'd, that he might stick
The small'st opinion on my least misuse?   5

Enter Iago and Emilia.

IAGO: What is your pleasure Madam?
How is 't with you?

DESDEMONA: I cannot tell: those that do teach young babes
Do it with gentle means, and easy tasks.   10
He might have chid me so: for in good faith
I am a child to chiding.

IAGO: What is the matter Lady?

EMILIA: Alas (Iago) my Lord hath so bewhor'd her,   15
Thrown such despite, and heavy terms upon her
That true heart cannot bear it.

DESDEMONA: Am I that name, Iago?

IAGO: What name (fair Lady)?

DESDEMONA: Such as she said my Lord did say I was.   20

EMILIA: He call'd her whore: a beggar in his drink
Could not have laid such terms upon his callet.

IAGO: Why did he so?

DESDEMONA: I do not know: I am sure I am none such.   25

IAGO: Do not weep, do not weep: alas the day.

EMILIA: Hath she forsook so many noble matches?
Her father? And her country? And her friends?
To be call'd whore? Would it not make one weep?

DESDEMONA: It is my wretched fortune.   30

IAGO: Beshrew him for 't:
How comes this trick upon him?

DESDEMONA: Nay, Heaven doth know.

EMILIA: I will be hang'd, if some eternal villain,
Some busy and insinuating rogue,
Some cogging, cozening slave, to get some office,
Have not devis'd this slander: I will be hang'd else.

5 IAGO: Fie, there is no such man: it is impossible.
DESDEMONA: If any such there be, Heaven pardon him.
EMILIA: A halter pardon him:
And hell gnaw his bones.
Why should he call her whore?
10 Who keeps her company?
What place? What time?
What form? What likelihood?
The Moor 's abus'd by some most villainous knave,
Some base notorious knave, some scurvy fellow.
15 Oh Heavens, that such companions thou 'ldst unfold,
And put in every honest hand a whip
To lash the rascals naked through the world,
Even from the East to th' West.
IAGO: Speak within door.
20 EMILIA: Oh fie upon them: some such squire he was
That turn'd your wit, the seamy side without,
And made you to suspect me with the Moor.
IAGO: You are a fool: go to.
DESDEMONA: Alas Iago,
25 What shall I do to win my Lord again?
Good friend, go to him: for by this light of Heaven,
I know not how I lost him. Here I kneel:
If e'er my will did trespass 'gainst his love,
Either in discourse of thought, or actual deed,
30 Or that mine eyes, mine ears, or any sense
Delighted them: or any other form.
Or that I do not yet, and ever did,
And ever will, (though he do shake me off

To beggarly divorcement) love him dearly,
Comfort forswear me. Unkindness may do much,
And his unkindness may defeat my life,
But never taint my love. I cannot say Whore,
It does abhor me now I speak the word,   5
To do the act, that might the addition earn,
Not the world's mass of vanity could make me.

IAGO: I pray you be content: 'tis but his humour.
The business of the State does him offence,
And he does chide with you.   10

DESDEMONA: If 'twere no other.

IAGO: It is but so, I warrant,
Hark how these instruments summon to supper:
And the messengers of Venice stays the meat,
Go in, and weep not: all things shall be well.   15
    Exeunt Desdemona and Emilia.
    Enter Roderigo.
How now Roderigo?

RODERIGO: I do not find
That thou deal'st justly with me.   20

IAGO: What in the contrary?

RODERIGO: Every day thou dafts me with some device
Iago, and rather, as it seems to me now, keep'st from
me all conveniency, than suppliest me with the least
advantage of hope: I will indeed no longer endure it. 25
Nor am I yet persuaded to put up in peace, what already
I have foolishly suffer'd.

IAGO: Will you hear me Roderigo?

RODERIGO: Faith I have heard too much, for your words
and performances are no kin together.   30

IAGO: You charge me most unjustly.

RODERIGO: With nought but truth: I have wasted myself
out of my means. The jewels you have had from me to

deliver Desdemona, would half have corrupted a votarist. You have told me she hath receiv'd them, and return'd me expectations and comforts of sudden respect, and acquaintance, but I find none.

5 IAGO: Well, go to: very well.

RODERIGO: Very well, go to: I cannot go to, (man) nor 'tis not very well. By this hand, I say it is scurvy: and begin to find myself fopp'd in it.

IAGO: Very well.

10 RODERIGO: I tell you, 'tis not very well: I will make myself known to Desdemona. If she will return me my jewels, I will give over my suit, and repent my unlawful solicitation. If not, assure yourself, I will seek satisfaction of you.

15 IAGO: You have said now.

RODERIGO: Ay: and said nothing but what I protest intendment of doing.

IAGO: Why, now I see there 's mettle in thee: and even from this instant do build on thee a better opinion
20 than ever before: give me thy hand Roderigo. Thou hast taken against me a most just exception: but yet I protest I have dealt most directly in thy affair.

RODERIGO: It hath not appear'd.

IAGO: I grant indeed it hath not appear'd: and your
25 suspicion is not without wit and judgement. But Roderigo, if thou hast that in thee indeed, which I have greater reason to believe now than ever (I mean purpose, courage, and valour) this night show it. If thou the next night following enjoy not Desdemona, take me
30 from this world with treachery, and devise engines for my life.

RODERIGO: Well: what is it? Is it within reason and compass?

IAGO: Sir, there is especial Commission come from Venice to depute Cassio in Othello's place.

RODERIGO: Is that true? Why then Othello and Desdemona return again to Venice.

IAGO: Oh no: he goes into Mauritania and taketh away 5 with him the fair Desdemona, unless his abode be linger'd here by some accident. Wherein none can be so determinate, as the removing of Cassio.

RODERIGO: How do you mean removing him?

IAGO: Why, by making him uncapable of Othello's place: 10 knocking out his brains.

RODERIGO: And that you would have me to do.

IAGO: Ay: if you dare do yourself a profit, and a right. He sups tonight with a harlotry: and thither will I go to him. He knows not yet of his honourable fortune: if you 15 will watch his going thence (which I will fashion to fall out between twelve and one) you may take him at your pleasure. I will near be to second your attempt, and he shall fall between us. Come, stand not amaz'd at it, but go along with me: I will show you such a necessity in 20 his death, that you shall think yourself bound to put it on him. It is now high supper time: and the night grows to waste. About it.

RODERIGO: I will hear further reason for this.

IAGO: And you shall be satisfied.   25

Exeunt.

IV. 3

Enter Othello, Lodovico, Desdemona, Emilia,
and Attendants.

LODOVICO: I do beseech you Sir, trouble yourself no 30 further.

OTHELLO: Oh pardon me: 'twill do me good to walk.

LODOVICO: Madam, good night: I humbly thank your
Ladyship.

DESDEMONA: Your Honour is most welcome.

5   OTHELLO: Will you walk Sir? Oh Desdemona.

DESDEMONA: My Lord.

OTHELLO: Get you to bed on th' instant, I will be return'd
forthwith: dismiss your attendant there: look 't be done.
Exeunt Othello, Lodovico, and Attendants.

10 DESDEMONA: I will my Lord.

EMILIA: How goes it now? He looks gentler than he did.

DESDEMONA: He says he will return incontinent,
And hath commanded me to go to bed,
And bid me to dismiss you.

15 EMILIA: Dismiss me?

DESDEMONA: It was his bidding: therefore good Emilia,
Give me my nightly wearing, and adieu.
We must not now displease him.

EMILIA: Ay, would you had never seen him.

20 DESDEMONA: So would not I: my love doth so approve
him,
That even his stubbornness, his checks, his frowns,
(Prithee unpin me) have grace and favour.

EMILIA: I have laid those sheets you bade me on the bed.

25 DESDEMONA: All 's one: good Father, how foolish are
our minds!
If I do die before, prithee shroud me
In one of these same sheets.

EMILIA: Come, come: you talk.

30 DESDEMONA: My Mother had a maid call'd Barbary,
She was in love: and he she lov'd prov'd mad,
And did forsake her. She had a song of willow,
An old thing 'twas: but it express'd her fortune,

And she died singing it. That song tonight,
Will not go from my mind: I have much to do,
But to go hang my head all at one side
And sing it like poor Barbary: prithee dispatch.
EMILIA: Shall I go fetch your night-gown?   5
DESDEMONA: No, unpin me here,
    This Lodovico is a proper man.
EMILIA: A very handsome man.
DESDEMONA: He speaks well.
EMILIA: I know a Lady in Venice would have walk'd   10
    barefoot to Palestine for a touch of his nether lip.
DESDEMONA: *The poor soul sat sighing, by a sycamore tree.*
    Sing all a green willow:
    Her hand on her bosom, her head on her knee,
    Sing willow, willow, willow.   15
    The fresh streams ran by her, and murmur'd her moans,
    Sing willow, &c.
    Her salt tears fell from her, and soften'd the stones,
    Sing willow, &c. (Lay by these)
    Willow, willow. (Prithee hie thee: he 'll come anon)   20
    Sing all a green willow must be my garland,
    Let nobody blame him, his scorn I approve.
    (Nay that 's not next). Hark, who is 't that knocks?
EMILIA: It 's the wind.
DESDEMONA: *I call'd my Love false Love: but what said he*   25
    then?
    Sing willow, &c.
    If I court mo women, you 'll couch with mo men.
    So get thee gone, good night: mine eyes do itch:
    Doth that bode weeping?   30
EMILIA: 'Tis neither here, nor there.
DESDEMONA: I have heard it said so. O these men, these
    men!

Dost thou in conscience think (tell me Emilia)
That there be women do abuse their husbands
In such gross kind?

EMILIA: There be some such, no question.

5 DESDEMONA: Wouldst thou do such a deed for all the
world?

EMILIA: Why, would not you?

DESDEMONA: No, by this heavenly light.

EMILIA: Nor I neither, by this heavenly light:
10 I might do 't as well i' th' dark.

DESDEMONA: Wouldst thou do such a deed for all the
world?

EMILIA: The world 's a huge thing:
It is a great price, for a small vice.

15 DESDEMONA: In troth, I think thou wouldst not.

EMILIA: In troth I think I should, and undo 't when I
had done. Marry, I would not do such a thing for a
joint ring, nor for measures of lawn, nor for gowns,
petticoats, nor caps, nor any petty exhibition. But for
20 all the whole world: 'uds pity, who would not make her
husband a cuckold, to make him a Monarch? I should
venture Purgatory for 't.

DESDEMONA: Beshrew me, if I would do such a wrong
For the whole world.

25 EMILIA: Why, the wrong is but a wrong i' th' world;
and having the world for your labour, 'tis a wrong in
your own world, and you might quickly make it right.

DESDEMONA: I do not think there is any such woman.

EMILIA: Yes, a dozen: and as many to th' vantage, as
30 would store the world they play'd for.
But I do think it is their husbands' faults
If wives do fall: (Say, that they slack their duties,
And pour our treasuries into foreign laps;

Or else break out in peevish jealousies,
Throwing restraint upon us: Or say they strike us,
Or scant our former having in despite)
Why we have galls: and though we have some grace,
Yet have we some revenge. Let husbands know,   5
Their wives have sense like them: They see, and smell,
And have their palates both for sweet, and sour,
As husbands have. What is it that they do,
When they change us for others? Is it sport?
I think it is: and doth affection breed it?   10
I think it doth. Is 't frailty that thus errs?
It is so too. And have not we affections?
Desires for sport? and frailty, as men have?
Then let them use us well: else let them know,
The ills we do, their ills instruct us so.   15
DESDEMONA: Good night, good night:
Heaven me such uses send,
Not to pick bad, from bad; but by bad, mend.
                    Exeunt.

V.1   20

Enter Iago, and Roderigo.
IAGO: Here, stand behind this bulk,
Straight will he come:
Wear thy good rapier bare, and put it home:
Quick, quick, fear nothing; I 'll be at thy elbow,   25
It makes us, or it mars us, think on that,
And fix most firm thy resolution.
RODERIGO: Be near at hand, I may miscarry in 't.
IAGO: Here, at thy hand: Be bold, and take thy stand.
RODERIGO: I have no great devotion to the deed,   30

And yet he hath given me satisfying reasons:
'Tis but a man gone. Forth my sword: he dies.

IAGO: I have rubb'd this young quat almost to the sense,
And he grows angry. Now, whether he kill Cassio,
5   Or Cassio him, or each do kill the other,
Every way makes my gain. Live Roderigo,
He calls me to a restitution large
Of gold, and jewels, that I bobb'd from him,
As gifts to Desdemona.
10 It must not be: If Cassio do remain,
He hath a daily beauty in his life,
That makes me ugly: and besides, the Moor
May unfold me to him: there stand I in much peril:
No, he must die. But so, I heard him coming.

15   *Enter Cassio.*

RODERIGO: I know his gait, 'tis he: villain thou diest.
CASSIO: That thrust had been mine enemy indeed,
But that my coat is better than thou know'st:
I will make proof of thine.
20   *[Stabs Roderigo.]*
RODERIGO: Oh, I am slain.
                    [Iago wounds Cassio from behind: exit.]
CASSIO: I am maim'd for ever:
Help hoa: murther, murther.
25   *Enter Othello.*
OTHELLO: The voice of Cassio, Iago keeps his word.
RODERIGO: O villain that I am.
OTHELLO: It is even so.
CASSIO: Oh help hoa: Light, a Surgeon.
30 OTHELLO: 'Tis he: O brave Iago, honest, and just,
That hast such noble sense of thy friend's wrong,
Thou teachest me. Minion, your dear lies dead,
And your unblest fate hies: Strumpet I come:

For of my heart, those charms thine eyes, are blotted:
Thy bed lust-stain'd, shall with lust's blood be spotted.
Exit Othello.
Enter Lodovico and Gratiano.

CASSIO: What hoa? no watch? No passage?   5
Murther, murther.

GRATIANO: 'Tis some mischance, the voice is very direful.

CASSIO: Oh help.

LODOVICO: Hark.

RODERIGO: Oh wretched villain.   10

LODOVICO: Two or three groan. 'Tis heavy night:
These may be counterfeits: Let 's think 't unsafe
To come into the cry, without more help.

RODERIGO: Nobody come: then shall I bleed to death.
Enter Iago.   15

LODOVICO: Hark.

GRATIANO: Here 's one comes in his shirt, with light,
and weapons.

IAGO: Who 's there?
Whose noise is this that cries on murther?   20

LODOVICO: We do not know.

IAGO: Do not you hear a cry?

CASSIO: Here, here: for heaven' sake help me.

IAGO: What 's the matter?

GRATIANO: This is Othello's Ancient, as I take it.   25

LODOVICO: The same indeed, a very valiant fellow.

IAGO: What are you here, that cry so grievously?

CASSIO: Iago? Oh I am spoil'd, undone by villains:
Give me some help.

IAGO: O me, Lieutenant!   30
What villains have done this?

CASSIO: I think that one of them is hereabout,
And cannot make away.

IAGO: Oh treacherous villains:
   What are you there? Come in, and give some help.
RODERIGO: O help me here.
CASSIO: That's one of them.
5 IAGO: Oh murd'rous slave! O villain! [*Stabs Roderigo.*]
RODERIGO: O damn'd Iago! O inhuman dog!
IAGO: Kill men i' th' dark?
   Where be these bloody thieves?
   How silent is this town! Hoa, murther, murther.
10   What may you be? Are you of good, or evil?
LODOVICO: As you shall prove us, praise us.
IAGO: Signior Lodovico?
LODOVICO: He sir.
IAGO: I cry you mercy: here's Cassio hurt by villains.
15 GRATIANO: Cassio?
IAGO: How is 't Brother?
CASSIO: My leg is cut in two.
IAGO: Marry heaven forbid:
   Light gentlemen, I'll bind it with my shirt.
20   *Enter Bianca.*
BIANCA: What is the matter hoa? Who is 't that cried?
IAGO: Who is 't that cried?
BIANCA: Oh my dear Cassio,
   My sweet Cassio: Oh Cassio, Cassio, Cassio.
25 IAGO: O notable strumpet. Cassio, may you suspect
   Who they should be, that have thus mangled you?
CASSIO: No.
GRATIANO: I am sorry to find you thus;
   I have been to seek you.
30 IAGO: Lend me a garter. So: — Oh for a chair.
   To bear him easily hence.
BIANCA: Alas he faints. Oh, Cassio, Cassio, Cassio.
IAGO: Gentlemen all, I do suspect this trash

To be a party in this injury.
Patience awhile, good Cassio. Come, come;
Lend me a light: know we this face, or no?
Alas my friend, and my dear countryman
Roderigo? No: Yes sure: Yes, 'tis Roderigo. 5

GRATIANO: What, of Venice?

IAGO: Even he sir: Did you know him?

GRATIANO: Know him? Ay.

IAGO: Signior Gratiano? I cry your gentle pardon:
These bloody accidents must excuse my manners, 10
That so neglected you.

GRATIANO: I am glad to see you.

IAGO: How do you Cassio? Oh, a chair, a chair.
[*Enter some with a chair.*]

GRATIANO: Roderigo? 15

IAGO: He, he, 'tis he:
Oh that's well said, the chair.
Some good man bear him carefully from hence,
I'll fetch the General's surgeon. For you Mistress,
Save you your labour. He that lies slain here (Cassio) 20
Was my dear friend. What malice was between you?

CASSIO: None in the world: nor do I know the man.

IAGO: What? look you pale? Oh bear him out o' th'
air.
Stay you good Gentlemen. Look you pale, Mistress? 25
Do you perceive the gastness of her eye?
Nay, if you stare, we shall hear more anon.
Behold her well: I pray you look upon her:
Do you see Gentlemen? Nay, guiltiness will speak
Though tongues were out of use. 30
Enter Emilia.

EMILIA: Alas, what is the matter?
What is the matter, husband?

IAGO: Cassio hath here been set on in the dark
  By Roderigo, and fellows that are 'scap'd:
  He's almost slain, and Roderigo quite dead.

EMILIA: Alas good Gentleman: alas good Cassio.

5 IAGO: This is the fruits of whoring. Prithee Emilia,
  Go know of Cassio where he supp'd tonight.
  What, do you shake at that?

BIANCA: He supp'd at my house, but I therefore shake
  not.

10 IAGO: O did he so? I charge you go with me.

EMILIA: Oh fie upon thee strumpet.

BIANCA: I am no strumpet, but of life as honest,
  As you that thus abuse me.

EMILIA: As I? Fie upon thee.

15 IAGO: Kind Gentlemen:
  Let's go see poor Cassio dress'd.
  Come Mistress, you must tell 's another tale.
  Emilia, run you to the Citadel,
  And tell my Lord and Lady, what hath happ'd:
20 Will you go on afore? This is the night
  That either makes me, or fordoes me quite.
                                        Exeunt.

V.2

Enter Othello with a light: Desdemona in her bed.

25 OTHELLO: It is the cause, it is the cause (my soul)
  Let me not name it to you, you chaste Stars,
  It is the cause. Yet I 'll not shed her blood,
  Nor scar that whiter skin of hers, than snow,
  And smooth as monumental alablaster:
30 Yet she must die, else she 'll betray more men:
  Put out the light, and then put out the light:

If I quench thee, thou flaming minister,
I can again thy former light restore,
Should I repent me. But once put out thy light,
Thou cunning'st pattern of excelling Nature,
I know not where is that Promethean heat   5
That can thy light re-lume.
When I have pluck'd thy rose,
I cannot give it vital growth again,
It needs must wither. I 'll smell thee on the tree.
Oh balmy breath, that dost almost persuade   10
Justice to break her sword. One more, one more:
Be thus when thou art dead, and I will kill thee,
And love thee after. One more, and that's the last.
So sweet, was ne'er so fatal. I must weep,
But they are cruel tears: This sorrow 's heavenly,   15
It strikes, where it doth love. She wakes.

DESDEMONA: Who 's there? Othello?

OTHELLO: Ay Desdemona.

DESDEMONA: Will you come to bed, my Lord?

OTHELLO: Have you pray'd tonight, Desdemona?   20

DESDEMONA: Ay my Lord

OTHELLO: If you bethink yourself of any crime
    Unreconcil'd as yet to Heaven, and Grace,
    Solicit for it straight.

DESDEMONA: Alack, my Lord,   25
    What may you mean by that?

OTHELLO: Well, do it, and be brief, I will walk by:
    I would not kill thy unprepared spirit,
    No, Heavens forfend, I would not kill thy soul.

DESDEMONA: Talk you of killing?   30

OTHELLO: Ay, I do.

DESDEMONA: Then Heaven have mercy on me.

OTHELLO: Amen, with all my heart.

DESDEMONA: If you say so, I hope you will not kill me.

OTHELLO: Humh.

DESDEMONA: And yet I fear you: for you are fatal then
When your eyes roll so.
5   Why I should fear, I know not,
Since guiltiness I know not: But yet I feel I fear.

OTHELLO: Think on thy sins.

DESDEMONA: They are loves I bear to you.

OTHELLO: Ay, and for that thou diest.

10 DESDEMONA: That death 's unnatural, that kills for
loving.
Alas, why gnaw you so your nether-lip?
Some bloody passion shakes your very frame:
These are portents: but yet I hope, I hope,
15   They do not point on me.

OTHELLO: Peace, and be still.

DESDEMONA: I will so: What 's the matter?

OTHELLO: That handkerchief
Which I so lov'd, and gave thee, thou gav'st to Cassio.

20 DESDEMONA: No by my life, and soul: send for the man,
And ask him.

OTHELLO: Sweet soul, take heed, take heed of perjury,
Thou art on thy death-bed.

DESDEMONA: Ay, but not yet to die.

25 OTHELLO: Presently.
Therefore confess thee freely of thy sin:
For to deny each article with oath,
Cannot remove, nor choke the strong conception
That I do groan withal. Thou art to die.

30 DESDEMONA: O Heaven have mercy on me.

OTHELLO: I say, Amen.

DESDEMONA: And have you mercy too. I never did
Offend you in my life: never lov'd Cassio,

But with such general warranty of Heaven,
As I might love. I never gave him token.

OTHELLO: By Heaven I saw my handkerchief in 's hand.
- O perjur'd woman, thou dost stone my heart,
And makes me call, what I intend to do,   5
A murther, which I thought a sacrifice.
I saw the handkerchief.

DESDEMONA: He found it then:
I never gave it him: Send, for him hither:
Let him confess a truth.   10

OTHELLO: He hath confess'd.

DESDEMONA: What, my Lord?

OTHELLO: That he hath us'd thee.

DESDEMONA: How? unlawfully?

OTHELLO: Ay.   15

DESDEMONA: He will not say so.

OTHELLO: No: his mouth is stopp'd:
Honest Iago hath ta'en order for 't.

DESDEMONA: Oh, my fear interprets. What is he dead?

OTHELLO: Had all his hairs been lives, my great revenge   20
Had stomach for them all.

DESDEMONA: Alas, he is betray'd, and I undone.

OTHELLO: Out strumpet: weep'st thou for him to my
     face?

DESDEMONA: O banish me, my Lord, but kill me not.   25

OTHELLO: Down strumpet.

DESDEMONA: Kill me tomorrow, let me live tonight.

OTHELLO: Nay, if you strive

DESDEMONA: But half an hour.

OTHELLO: Being done, there is no pause.   30

DESDEMONA: But while I say one prayer.

OTHELLO: It is too late.   *Smothers her.*
                    Emilia calls at the door.

EMILIA: My Lord, my Lord? What hoa?
My Lord, my Lord.

OTHELLO: What noise is this? Not dead? not yet quite
dead?

5   I that am cruel, am yet merciful,
I would not have thee linger in thy pain.
So, so.

EMILIA *within:* What hoa? My Lord, my Lord?

OTHELLO: Who's there?

10   EMILIA: Oh good my Lord, I would speak a word with
you.

OTHELLO: Yes: 'Tis Emilia: by and by. She's dead.
'Tis like she comes to speak of Cassio's death:
The noise was high. Hah, no more moving?

15   Still as the grave. Shall she come in? Were't good?
I think she stirs again. No, what's best to do?
If she come in, she'll sure speak to my wife:
My wife, my wife: what wife? I have no wife.
Oh insupportable! Oh heavy hour!

20   Methinks, it should be now a huge eclipse
Of Sun, and Moon; and that th' affrighted Globe
Did yawn at alteration.

EMILIA: I do beseech you
That I may speak with you. Good my Lord.

25   OTHELLO: I had forgot thee: oh, come in Emilia.
Soft, by and by, let me the curtains draw.
Where art thou? What's the matter with thee now?
                    Enter Emilia.

EMILIA: Oh my good Lord, yonder's foul murthers done.

30   OTHELLO: What? now?

EMILIA: But now, my Lord.

OTHELLO: It is the very error of the Moon,
She comes more nearer Earth than she was wont,

And makes men mad.

EMILIA: Cassio, my Lord, hath kill'd
A young Venetian, call'd Roderigo.

OTHELLO: Roderigo kill'd? and Cassio kill'd?

EMILIA: No, Cassio is not kill'd. 5

OTHELLO: Not Cassio kill'd? Then murther 's out of tune,
And sweet revenge grows harsh.

DESDEMONA: O falsely, falsely murder'd.

EMILIA: Alas! what cry is that? 10

OTHELLO: That? What?

EMILIA: Out and alas, that was my Lady's voice.
Help, help hoa, help. Oh Lady speak again,
Sweet Desdemona, oh sweet Mistress, speak.

DESDEMONA: A guiltless death, I die, 15

EMILIA: Oh who hath done this deed?

DESDEMONA: Nobody: I myself, farewell:
Commend me to my kind Lord: oh farewell. *She dies.*

OTHELLO: Why, how should she be murder'd?

EMILIA: Alas: who knows? 20

OTHELLO: You hear her say herself, it was not I.

EMILIA: She said so: I must needs report the truth.

OTHELLO: She's like a liar gone to burning hell,
'Twas I that kill'd her.

EMILIA: Oh the more Angel she, and you the blacker 25
Devil.

OTHELLO: She turn'd to folly: and she was a whore.

EMILIA: Thou dost belie her, and thou art a devil.

OTHELLO: She was false as water.

EMILIA: Thou art rash as fire, to say 30
That she was false. Oh she was heavenly true.

OTHELLO: Cassio did top her: Ask thy husband else.
O, I were damn'd beneath all depth in hell:

But that I did proceed upon just grounds
To this extremity. Thy husband knew it all.

EMILIA: My husband?

OTHELLO: Thy husband.

5   EMILIA: That she was false to wedlock?

OTHELLO: Ay, with Cassio: had she been true,
If Heaven would make me such another world,
Of one entire and perfect chrysolite,
I 'ed not have sold her for it.

10 EMILIA: My husband?

OTHELLO: Ay, 'twas he that told me on her first.
An honest man he is, and hates the slime
That sticks on filthy deeds.

EMILIA: My husband?

15 OTHELLO: What needs this iterance, woman?
I say, thy husband.

EMILIA: Oh Mistress,
Villainy hath made mocks with love:
My husband say she was false?

20 OTHELLO: He, woman;
I say thy husband: Dost understand the word?
My friend, thy husband; honest, honest Iago.

EMILIA: If he say so, may his pernicious soul
Rot half a grain a day: he lies to th' heart,

25 She was too fond of her most filthy bargain.

OTHELLO: Hah?

EMILIA: Do thy worst:
This deed of thine is no more worthy Heaven,
Than thou wast worthy her.

30 OTHELLO: Peace, you were best.

EMILIA: Thou hast not half that power to do me harm,
As I have to be hurt. Oh gull, oh dolt,
As ignorant as dirt: thou hast done a deed

(I care not for thy sword) I 'll make thee known,
Though I lost twenty lives. Help, help, hoa, help:
The Moor hath kill'd my Mistress. Murther, murther.
   Enter Montano, Gratiano, and Iago.

MONTANO: What is the matter? How now General?   5

EMILIA: Oh, are you come, Iago: you have done well,
 That men must lay their murthers on your neck.

GRATIANO: What is the matter?

EMILIA: Disprove this villain, if thou be'st a man:
 He says, thou told'st him that his wife was false: 10
 I know thou didst not: thou 'rt not such a villain.
 Speak, for my heart is full.

IAGO: I told him what I thought,
 And told no more
 Than what he found himself was apt, and true. 15

EMILIA: But did you ever tell him,
 She was false?

IAGO: I did.

EMILIA: You told a lie, an odious damned lie:
 Upon my soul, a lie; a wicked lie. 20
 She false with Cassio?
 Did you say with Cassio?

IAGO: With Cassio, Mistress!
 Go to, charm your tongue.

EMILIA: I will not charm my tongue; 25
 I am bound to speak,
 My Mistress here lies murthered in her bed.

ALL: Oh Heavens, forfend.

EMILIA: And your reports have set the murder on.

OTHELLO: Nay stare not Masters, 30
 It is true indeed.

GRATIANO: 'Tis a strange truth.

MONTANO: O monstrous act.

EMILIA: Villainy, villainy, villainy:
　　I think upon 't, I think: I smell 't: O villainy:
　　I thought so then: I 'll kill myself for grief.
　　O villainy! villainy!
5 IAGO: What, are you mad?
　　I charge you get you home.
EMILIA: Good Gentlemen, let me have leave to speak:
　　'Tis proper I obey him: but not now:
　　Perchance Iago, I will ne'er go home.
10　　　　　　*Othello falls on the bed.*
OTHELLO: Oh, oh, oh.
EMILIA: Nay, lay thee down, and roar:
　　For thou hast kill'd the sweetest innocent,
　　That e'er did lift up eye.
15 OTHELLO: Oh she was foul!
　　I scarce did know you Uncle, there lies your niece,
　　Whose breath (indeed) these hands have newly stopp'd:
　　I know this act shows horrible and grim.
GRATIANO: Poor Desdemon:
20　　I am glad thy Father 's dead,
　　Thy match was mortal to him: and pure grief
　　Shore his old thread in twain. Did he live now,
　　This sight would make him do a desperate turn:
　　Yea, curse his better Angel from his side,
25　　And fall to reprobance.
OTHELLO: 'Tis pitiful: but yet Iago knows
　　That she with Cassio, hath the act of shame,
　　A thousand times committed. Cassio confess'd it,
　　And she did gratify his amorous works
30　　With that recognizance and pledge of love
　　Which I first gave her: I saw it in his hand:
　　It was a handkerchief, an antique token
　　My Father gave my Mother.

EMILIA: Oh God! heavenly God!

IAGO: 'Zounds, hold your peace.

EMILIA: 'Twill out, 'twill out. I peace?
No, I will speak as liberal as the North;
Let Heaven, and men, and devils, let them all,   5
All, all, cry shame against me, yet I 'll speak.

IAGO: Be wise, and get you home.

EMILIA: I will not.

GRATIANO: Fie, Your sword upon a woman.

EMILIA: Oh thou dull Moor,   10
That handkerchief thou speak'st of
I found by fortune, and did give my husband:
For often, with a solemn earnestness,
(More than indeed belong'd to such a trifle)
He begg'd of me, to steal 't.   15

IAGO: Villainous whore.

EMILIA: She give it Cassio? No, alas I found it,
And I did give 't my husband.

IAGO: Filth, thou liest.

EMILIA: By Heaven I do not, I do not Gentlemen?   20
Oh murd'rous coxcomb, what should such a fool
Do with so good a wife?

OTHELLO: Are there no stones in Heaven,
But what serves for the thunder?
Precious villain.   25

[*The Moor runs at Iago. Iago kills his wife.*]

GRATIANO: The woman falls:
Sure he hath kill'd his wife.

Exit Iago

EMILIA: Ay, ay: oh lay me by my Mistress' side.   30

GRATIANO: He 's gone, but his wife 's kill'd.

MONTANO: 'Tis a notorious villain: take you this weapon

Which I have here recover'd from the Moor:
Come guard the door without, let him not pass,
But kill him rather. I 'll after that same villain,
For 'tis a damned slave.

5   *Exit.*

OTHELLO: I am not valiant neither:
But every puny whipster gets my sword.
But why should honour outlive honesty?
Let it go all.

10 EMILIA: What did thy song bode Lady?
Hark, canst thou hear me? I will play the swan,
And die in music: *Willow, willow, willow.*
Moor, she was chaste: She lov'd thee, cruel Moor,
So come my soul to bliss, as I speak true:

15 So speaking as I think, alas, I die.   *She dies.*

OTHELLO: I have another weapon in this chamber,
It was a sword of Spain, the ice brook's temper:
Oh here it is: Uncle I must come forth.

GRATIANO: If thou attempt it, it will cost thee dear;

20 Thou hast no weapon, and perforce must suffer.

OTHELLO: Look in upon me then, and speak with me,
Or naked as I am I will assault thee.

GRATIANO: What is the matter?

OTHELLO: Behold, I have a weapon:

25 A better never did itself sustain
Upon a soldier's thigh. I have seen the day,
That with this little arm, and this good sword,
I have made my way through more impediments
Than twenty times your stop. But (oh vain boast)

30 Who can control his Fate? 'Tis not so now.
Be not afraid, though you do see me weapon'd:
Here is my journey's end, here is my butt
And very sea-mark of my utmost sail.

Do you go back dismay'd? 'Tis a lost fear:
Man but a rush against Othello's breast,
And he retires. Where should Othello go?
Now: how dost thou look now? Oh ill-starr'd wench,
Pale as thy smock: when we shall meet at compt,   5
This looks of thine will hurl my soul from Heaven,
And fiends will snatch at it. Cold, cold, my girl?
Even like thy chastity. O cursed, cursed slave!
Whip me ye devils
From the possession of this heavenly sight: 10
Blow me about in winds, roast me in sulphur,
Wash me in steep-down gulfs of liquid fire:
Oh Desdemon! dead Desdemon: dead. Oh, oh!
        Enter Lodovico, Montano, Iago, and Officers:
                Cassio in a chair.   15
LODOVICO: Where is this rash, and most unfortunate
    man?
OTHELLO: That 's he that was Othello: here I am.
LODOVICO: Where is that viper?
    Bring the villain forth.   20
OTHELLO: I look down towards his feet; but that 's a
    fable,
    If that thou be'st a Devil, I cannot kill thee.
LODOVICO: Wrench his sword from him.
IAGO: I bleed Sir, but not kill'd.   25
OTHELLO: I am not sorry neither, I 'ld have thee live:
    For in my sense, 'tis happiness to die.
LODOVICO: Oh thou Othello, that was once so good,
    Fall'n in the practice of a cursed slave,
    What shall be said to thee.   30
OTHELLO: Why any thing:
    An honourable murderer, if you will:
    For nought I did in hate, but all in honour.

LODOVICO: This wretch hath part confess'd his villainy:
Did you and he consent in Cassio's death.

OTHELLO: Ay.

CASSIO: Dear General, I never gave you cause.

5 OTHELLO: I do believe it, and I ask your pardon:
Will you, I pray, demand that demi-devil,
Why he hath thus ensnar'd my soul and body?

IAGO: Demand me nothing: what you know, you know:
From this time forth, I never will speak word.

10 LODOVICO: What? not to pray?

GRATIANO: Torments will ope your lips.

OTHELLO: Well, thou dost best.

LODOVICO: Sir,
You shall understand what hath befall'n,
15 (Which, as I think, you know not) here is a letter
Found in the pocket of the slain Roderigo,
And here another, the one of them imports
The death of Cassio, to be undertook
By Roderigo.

20 OTHELLO: O villain!

CASSIO: Most heathenish, and most gross.

LODOVICO: Now, here 's another discontented paper
Found in his pocket too: and this it seems,
Roderigo meant t' have sent this damned villain:
25 But that (belike) Iago in the interim
Came in, and satisfied him.

OTHELLO: Oh thou pernicious caitiff;
How came you (Cassio) by that handkerchief
That was my wife's?

30 CASSIO: I found it in my chamber:
And he himself confess'd it but even now,
That there he dropp'd it for a special purpose,
Which wrought to his desire.

OTHELLO: O fool, fool, fool!

CASSIO: There is besides, in Roderigo's letter,
How he upbraids Iago, that he made him
Brave me upon the watch: whereon it came
That I was cast: and even but now he spake   5
(After long seeming dead) Iago hurt him,
Iago set him on.

LODOVICO: You must forsake this room, and go with us:
Your power, and your command is taken off,
And Cassio rules in Cyprus. For this slave,   10
If there be any cunning cruelty,
That can torment him much, and hold him long,
It shall be his. You shall close prisoner rest,
Till that the nature of your fault be known
To the Venetian State. Come, bring away.   15

OTHELLO: Soft you; a word or two before you go:
I have done the State some service, and they know 't:
No more of that. I pray you in your letters,
When you shall these unlucky deeds relate,
Speak of me, as I am. Nothing extenuate,   20
Nor set down aught in malice.
Then you must speak,
Of one that lov'd not wisely, but too well:
Of one, not easily jealous, but being wrought,
Perplex'd in the extreme: Of one, whose hand   25
(Like the base Indian) threw a pearl away
Richer than all his tribe: Of one, whose subdu'd eyes,
Albeit unused to the melting mood,
Drops tears as fast as the Arabian trees
Their medicinable gum. Set you down this: 30
And say besides, that in Aleppo once,
Where a malignant, and a turban'd Turk
Beat a Venetian, and traduc'd the State,

I took by th' throat the circumcised dog,
And smote him, thus.
                    He stabs himself.
LODOVICO: Oh bloody period.
5 GRATIANO: All that is spoke, is marr'd.
   OTHELLO: I kiss'd thee, ere I kill'd thee: No way but this
   Killing myself, to die upon a kiss.   *Dies.*
   CASSIO: This did I fear, but thought he had no weapon:
   For he was great of heart.
10 LODOVICO: Oh Spartan dog:
   More fell than anguish, hunger, or the sea:
   Look on the tragic loading of this bed:
   This is thy work:
   The object poisons sight,
15 Let it be hid. Gratiano, keep the house,
   And seize upon the fortunes of the Moor,
   For they succeed on you. To you, Lord Governor,
   Remains the censure of this hellish villain:
   The time, the place, the torture, oh inforce it:
20 Myself will straight aboard, and to the State,
   This heavy act, with heavy heart relate.
                    Exeunt.

NOTES

References are to the page and line of this edition;
there are 33 lines to the full page.

The Names of the Actors: This list is given in the Folio   P. 22
at the end of the text.

Off-capped: stood cap in hand.   P. 23 L. 14

bumbast circumstance: stuffed out excuse. *Bumbast:*   P. 23 L. 17
cotton wool padding.

epithets of war: military arguments.   P. 23 L. 18

great arithmetician: contemporary books on military   P. 23 L. 22
service were full of elaborate diagrams and numerals
to explain military formations. Cassio is a student of
such books.

a fellow ... fair wife: A much-disputed phrase.   P. 23 L. 24
There is an Italian proverb: 'You have married a
fair wife? You are damned.' If Iago has this in mind,
he means that Cassio is about to marry.

division of a battle: organization of an army.   P. 23 L. 26

bookish theoric: military theorist, a student, not a   P. 23 L. 27
practical soldier.

toged: wearing a toga; this is the Quarto reading;   P. 23 L. 28
the Folio reads *tongued*. *Consuls:* councillors.

And I ... had seen the proof: Iago's complaint that a   P. 24 L. 1
mere book soldier had been promoted over his head
was not uncommon at this time when there was no
regular army and promotion and appointment depended solely on the partiality of the General. A
notable instance occurred in the Islands Voyage of
1597. In the previous year Sir Francis Vere (a general
of great experience) had been the Earl of Essex's
chief military officer and was mainly responsible for
the capture of Cadiz. The next year Lord Mountjoy,
who was noted as a 'bookish soldier', was promoted
over Vere's head. Vere relates in his *Commentaries*
that he was so offended that he refused to take any
action in the deliberations of the Council of War.

P. 24 L. 3   *be-leed:* have the wind taken out of my sails.

P. 24 L. 4   *counter-caster:* one who calculates by counters, i.e., arithmetician.

P. 24 LL. 5–6   *Lieutenant . . . Ancient:* the three officers in a company were the captain (commanding), the lieutenant, and the ancient (or ensign).

P. 24 L. 6   *God bless the mark:* an exclamation of impatience.

P. 24 L. 11   *letter:* private recommendation.

P. 24 L. 12   *old gradation:* the old rule of seniority.

P. 24 L. 24   *cashier'd:* dismissed. The word at this time did not imply dishonourable discharge.

P. 24 L. 26   *trimm'd . . . duty:* wearing outwardly the form and appearance of loyalty.

P. 24 L. 31   *themselves homage:* serve themselves. *Homage:* an outward sign of service.

P. 25 L. 10   *For daws to peck at:* for any chattering fool to mock me.

P. 25   *though . . . colour:* cause him some annoyance by
LL. 17–19   tarnishing his joy.

P. 27 L. 2   *gennets for germans:* ponies for family relations. A gennet was a small Moorish horse.

P. 27 L. 13   *odd even:* i.e., about midnight.

P. 27 L. 26   *extravagant, and wheeling:* vagabond and wheedling.

P. 28 L. 17   *Sagittary:* No building of this name is known to have existed in Venice.

P. 30 LL. 1–2   *voice . . . as the Duke's:* a vote equally powerful with the Duke's.

P. 30 L. 7   *Signiory:* the governing body of Venice.

P. 30   *my demerits . . . (unbonneted):* 'My deserts are equal
LL. 11–12   to my Fortune.' A difficult phrase, for 'unbonneted' would naturally mean 'without a cap', i.e., in the posture of an inferior: *Shakespeare,* however, uses 'bonnet' in *Coriolanus* (II. ii. 30) in the sense of 're-moving the cap', and so 'unbonneted' may equally mean 'with the cap on'. There is a similar double use today of 'to cap'.

haste, post-haste: with the quickest possible speed. P. 30 L. 30
When it was necessary to urge the post-boy to
greater speed than usual the letter was endorsed
'haste, post haste'. The Earl of Essex on occasion
inscribed his letters 'haste, haste, haste, haste post
haste, haste for life'.

galleys: the fastest of all vessels. The galley carried P. 31 L. 1
sails and was also rowed with oars manned by slaves.

carrack: the largest of the Spanish merchant vessels P. 31 L. 14
trading with South America and the Indies. A very
rich carrack, the *Madre de Dios,* was captured by
English sailors in 1592, with so large a cargo of pepper that the pepper trade was dislocated for years.
Even after the sailors had stolen most of the portable
loot, the remainder fetched £150,000. In 1602
another carrack, the *St Valentine,* was taken: its
booty fetched more than £25,000.

disputed on: argued in the Courts. P. 32 L. 14

I therefore apprehend ...: Brabantio's wild charges P. 32 L. 16
are not so foolish as they appear to modern readers.
According to accepted Elizabethan ideas, Desdemona as a lady of high birth should marry with one
of her rank and with the approval of her father and
family: that she should elope with a stranger, and a
Moor at that, is so unthinkable and unnatural that
Brabantio can only suppose that she is the victim of
witchcraft.

out of warrant: unlawful. P. 32 L. 18

fit time ... direct Session: the ordinary sessions at P. 32
which witches and other criminals are tried. LL. 26–7

I. 3.: This episode, with post after post galloping to P. 33 L. 12
Court from the West, was several times enacted in
real life in the months before *Othello* was written.
In 1597 there was great alarm that a Spanish Fleet
was at sea. The fleet was actually within two days'
sail of Cornwall when it was scattered by a tempest.
In 1599 there was another alarm with many con-
tradictory rumours which caused a large defence
force to be concentrated around London.

P. 33 L. 24   *bearing up to :* making course for.

P. 33 L. 27   *main article :* general purport.

P. 34 L. 7   *assay of reason :* reasonable test.

P. 34 L. 12   *more . . . bear it :* more easily take it.

P. 35 L. 14   *general care :* public business.

P. 35 L. 16   *flood-gate :* like flood water passing through an opened sluice.

P. 35 L. 24   *mountebanks :* quack doctors who dealt in dubious drugs.

P. 36 L. 22   *round unvarnish'd tale :* simple, unadorned account.

P. 36   *motion . . . herself :* she was so shy that she blushed at
LL. 29–30 any undertaking.

P. 37 L. 11   *modern seeming :* slight suspicion.

P. 38 L. 8   *most disastrous chances :* Othello's story of his adventures is very like a similar tale which caused great wonder and gossip in 1599 and later. John Chamberlain, a writer of gossip and news, wrote on 17th January, 1599, 'The news comes now very hot that Sebastian the king of Portingale, that was said to be slain in the battle in Barbary, is at Venice, and hath made so good trial of himself that the Venetians allow him, and maintain almost four-score persons about him at their charge. They say he tells very strange stories, how he with fourteen more escaped from the battle, and got up into the mountains, and so, by many adventures, he went and he went till he came into Ethiopia, or Prester John's land, meaning from thence to have gone into the East Indies, but, understanding that they were yielded and sworn to the King of Spain, durst not proceed, but turned back again, and *per tot discrimina* in this long pilgrimage (wherein he hath been taken, bought, and sold twelve or thirteen times), got at last to Venice, where he tells them all that was negotiated twixt him and them either by letters or ambassadors since he was of any good remembrance, and that with so many particulars as are thought infallible testimonies.' Accounts of this Sebastian's adventures were printed in 1602.

heads . . . beneath their shoulders: This marvel was re-   P. 38
ported by Sir Walter Ralegh in his account of his   LL. 18–19
expedition to Guiana of 1595. 'Next unto Arui there
are two rivers Atoica and Caora, and on that branch
which is called Caora, are a nation of people, whose
heads appear not above their shoulders . . . they are
called Ewaipanoma: they are reported to have their
eyes in their shoulders, and their mouths in the
middle of their breasts, and that a long train of hair
groweth backward between their shoulders.'
[Hakluyt's *Voyages*, Everyman Edn. vii, 328].

beguile her of: draw from her.   P. 38 L. 30

lay a sentence: quote a proverbial saying.   P. 40 L. 12

When remedies . . . through the ear: This rhymed   P. 40
passage is notable, for it draws attention to the   LL. 14–31
wronged father. Shakespeare in *Othello* is very
subtle in his varying rhythms. For the speech of
grave persons blank verse is the natural medium.
Prose denotes a more familiar tone. Othello usually
speaks in verse except where his emotion gets the
better of his reason. Iago, on the other hand, speaks
prose when he is outwardly the jocular 'honest
Iago', but when moved to emotion, genuine in his
soliloquies, or feigned as when he affects indignation,
he speaks verse.

When remedies . . . depended: Anxiety ends when   P. 40
the feared event happens.   LL. 14–15

So let the Turk . . . ear: Brabantio retaliates with   P. 40
a few 'sentences' of his own. 'If we smile at the   LL. 22–31
loss of Cyprus, of course the loss is trifling. A man
who can take comfort from sententious consolations
is indeed patient, for he has not only to endure easy
consolation but the grief as well. These proverbs
work both ways: mere words hurt no one.'

opinion . . . effects: your reputation is such that we   P. 41 LL 3–4
shall feel safer.

That I did love . . . my Lord: 'my love for the Moor   P. 41
is publicly shown by the way in which I have vio-   LL. 29–32
lently taken up my fortune with my own hands,
for I have become a warrior like my husband.'

P. 42 L. 4   *A moth of peace:* a useless creature, living at home.

P. 42   *Nor to comply ... satisfaction:* A much disputed pas-
LL. 11–12   sage, though the general sense is clear – 'I am no
             longer a young man: I did not marry Desdemona
             through wanton desire'.

P. 42 L. 18 *speculative, and offic'd instrument:* 'my intelligence
             and efficiency,' lit., my powers of sight and action.

P. 42 L. 22 *Make . . . . against:* overcome.

P. 43 LL. 7–8 *If virtue ... than black:* If his worthiness is con-
             sidered, your son-in-law, though black, is not with-
             out a pleasing beauty.

P. 43 L. 10 *Look to her (Moor):* Iago, in the background, ob-
             serves these words and later reminds Othello of
             them with deadly effect.

P. 43 L. 19 *obey the time:* yield to necessity.

P. 44 L. 18 *sect: sect* (set), and *scion,* mean the same, – a slip
             taken from a plant or tree, and planted to produce a
             new growth.

P. 44 L. 27 *defeat thy favour:* disguise your face.

P. 44 L. 31 *answerable sequestration:* as violent reaction.

P. 45 L. 1   *luscious as locusts:* it is not known what fruit bore
             this name.

P. 45 L. 2   *coloquintida:* bitter cucumber, used as a purge.

P. 46 L. 12 *smooth dispose:* disposition easy.

P. 46 L. 25 *high wrought flood:* heavy sea.

P. 47 L. 1   *hold the mortise:* remain fast joined.

P. 47 LL. 6–7 *Bear ... th' ever-fixed Pole:* the bright stars in the
             'tail' of Ursa Major.

P. 48 LL. 4–5 *make the main ... regard:* until we can no longer
             distinguish between sea and sky.

P. 48 L. 16 *approv'd allowance:* proved skill.

P. 48 L. 18 *stand ... cure:* have every hope of cure, i.e., fulfil-
             ment.

P. 49 LL. 1–2 *in th' essential ... tire the ingeniver:* i.e., She is so
             perfect a creature that one who would essay to
             depict her wearies in the effort. The word *ingeniver*

is not found elsewhere; it means presumably 'ingenious poet'. Shakespeare however often invents such words. Some editors emend to 'ingener'. The Quarto reads 'Does bear all excellency'.

bold show of courtesy: Here Cassio kisses Emilia – P. 50 L. 12 a mark of easy familiarity which shows that Cassio regards himself as of superior social rank to the Ancient.

pictures out of door: i.e., painted – and dumb – in P. 50 L. 23 company.

bells in your parlours: i.e., ever giving tongue at home. P. 50 L. 24

vouch . . . malice itself: one whom even the malicious P. 51 would praise.   LL. 31–2

cod's head for the salmon's tail: to prefer the tail-end P. 52 L. 7 of a good thing to the head of an indifferent. *Cod's head:* a fool.

chronicle small beer: make a fuss of trifles.   P. 52 L. 12

He takes her by the palm: Shakespeare does not bur- P. 52 L. 19 den his plays with elaborate stage directions in the manner of modern dramatists, but the action is often minutely indicated in the dialogue.

set . . . pegs: 'make you sing in a different key.' P. 53 *to set the pegs:* to tune (an instrument).   LL. 24–5

prattle . . . fashion: talk idly.   P. 53 L. 32

watches on the Court of Guard: is on duty with the P. 54 L. 11 guard. The Court of Guard is both the guard itself and the guard-room.

finger thus: i.e., on the lips.   P. 54 L. 14

on the devil: for the Devil was painted as a black P. 54 L. 19 man.

heave the gorge: retch.   P. 54 L. 25

trace: follow. Some editors amend to *trash:* restrain. P. 56 L. 26

right garb: The Quarto reads *rank garb:* lustful man- P. 56 L. 29 ner, i.e., of being Desdemona's lover.

pottle-deep: to the bottom of the pottle (which P. 59 L 10 holds two quarts).

P 59 L. 12   *in a wary distance:* 'encourage easy familiarity, and so are easy to take offence.'

P. 59 L. 20   *If . . . dream:* if my dream is fulfilled by what follows.

P. 60 L. 5   *sweats not:* i.e., without effort.

P. 60 L. 11   *King Stephen . . . peer:* An old and popular English ballad.

P. 61 L. 8   *platform:* level place where the cannon were mounted.

P. 61 L. 13   *just equinox:* an exact equal.

P. 61 L. 20   *horologe . . . set:* 'the clock round twice.'

P. 62 L. 11   *twiggen bottle:* a bottle encased in wickerwork.

P. 63 L. 9   *upon his motion:* if he moves.

P. 63 L. 17   *some planet:* to those who believe in astrology disasters were attributed to the evil influence of planets.

P. 63 L. 30   *spend your rich opinion:* lose your good reputation.

P. 64 L. 21   *If partially . . . in office:* If you allow yourself to be bound by partiality or because he is your fellow officer.

P. 66 L. 11   *imposition:* a quality laid on a man by others.

P. 69 L. 10   *fills up the cry:* In Elizabethan times a pack of hounds was not of uniform breed but so chosen that their cry made a musical harmony. When King James I first came to England in 1603 'from Stamford Hill to London was made a train with a tame deer, with such twinings and doubles, that the hound could not take it faster than his Majesty proceeded; yet still, by the industry of the huntsman, and the subtlety of him that made the train in a full-mouthed cry all the way, never farther distant than one close from the highway, whereby his Majesty rid, and for the most part directly against his Majesty, whom, together with the whole company, had the lee wind from the hounds, to the end they might the better perceive and judge of the uniformity in the cries'. [Nichols' *Progresses of King James,* i. 139].

P. 70 L. 6   *bid, good morrow General:* It was a common custom to play or sing a song in the early morning to distinguished visitors or to a newly wedded couple on the night after their wedding.

A Florentine more kind: i.e., one of my countrymen: P. 71 L. 17
Iago is a Venetian.

occasion by the front: as the proverb goes, 'take Time P. 71 L. 28
by the forelock'.

your bosom: what is in your heart. P. 72 L. 3

in strangeness . . . politic distance: his coldness to you P. 73 LL. 4–5
shall only be so much as his official position demands.

present reconciliation take: be reconciled to him at P. 74 L. 11
once.

Cassio, That came a-wooing; This is the first indica- P. 75 LL. 6–7
tion that Cassio has known Desdemona before her
marriage. There is indeed an inconsistency in the
relationship between Cassio, Desdemona, and Othello which cannot be logically explained. The times of
the various events in the earlier acts of the play are
definitely stated. Othello takes Desdemona away
from Brabantio's house and marries her. Immedi-
ately afterwards, before the consummation of his
wedding, he is sent away to Cyprus. Desdemona re-
joins him and the interrupted marriage is completed.
That same night Cassio is made drunk on guard and
cashiered. Next morning Cassio begs Desdemona to
sue for him, and at once Iago begins to poison
Othello's mind. Where then was there any time or
opportunity for Desdemona's supposed familiarities
with Cassio? The difficulty is obvious in reading the
play, but not noticed when the play is acted.

dilations: expressions, revelations. The Quarto reads P. 77 L. 8
'denotements'.

Keep leets . . . sessions sit: i.e., mingle on solemn P. 77 L. 28
occasions. *Leets:* manorial courts.

mock . . . feeds on: i.e., jealousy is both fed and P. 78
tormented by suspicion. LL. 25–6

cuckold . . . his wronger: the cuckold who dislikes P. 78
his wife and knows her falseness is not tormented LL. 26–7
by suspicious jealousy.

P. 78 L. 32   *riches fineless:* unbounded wealth.

P. 79 L. 9   *exsufflicate:* blown up, (spelt 'exufflicate' in Quarto
               and Folio).

P. 79 L. 29   *In Venice:* Venice was notorious for the looseness of
               its women: Venetian courtesans were one of the
               sights of Europe.

P. 80 L. 1   *deceive her father:* An echo of Brabantio's parting
               words, p. 43 l. 10-11.

P. 80 L. 7   *seel . . . up:* blind. A technical term used in falconry.
               When wild hawks were caught a thread was passed
               through their eyelids which were thus 'seeled' until
               they were used to the hood.

P. 81 L. 10   *match . . . forms:* compare you with her country-
               men (of her own colour).

P. 81 L. 26   *strain his entertainment:* urge his appointment.

P. 82 LL. 2-3 *learn'd . . . dealings:* with wide experience of human
               nature.

P. 82 L. 4   *jesses:* straps by which a hawk's legs were secured.

P. 82 L. 8   *chamberers:* gallants who haunt ladies' chambers.

P. 82 L. 19   *forked plague:* i.e., horns. Cuckolds were supposed
               to wear invisible horns.

P. 83 L. 12   *work ta'en out:* the pattern copied.

P. 84 L. 7   *Be not acknown on 't:* have no knowledge of it.

P. 85 L. 5   *Pioners:* labourers in the army, pioneers, considered
               the lowest of the soldiers.

P. 85 L. 14   *mortal engines:* i.e., cannon. *Mortal:* deadly.

P. 86 L. 3   *God buy you:* God be with you: good-bye.

P. 87 L. 2   *salt . . . pride:* as eager as she-wolves on heat.

P. 88 L. 20   *Pontic Sea:* the Black Sea. In Philemon Holland's
               translation of Pliny's *History of the World,* 1601, Bk.
               II, Chap. 97, it is noted that 'the Sea Pontus ever-
               more floweth and runneth out into Propontis, but
               the Sea never retireth back again within Pontus'.

P. 90 LL. 5-6 *be edified by report:* Desdemona falls into the clown's
               foolery and answers him with high-flown phrases.
               Edified being a clerical phrase, back comes another.

crusadoes: Portuguese coins worth about a crown.   P. 90 L. 19

hand is moist: A hot moist palm was supposed to   P. 91 L. 3
denote desire.

hearts of old ... hands, not hearts: This passage has   P. 91
been taken as a reference to the order of baronets,   LL. 14–15
created by James I in 1611, who bore on their
heraldic coats of arms 'the bloody hand of Ulster':
if so, the lines are a later addition: but the reference
is very doubtful. The antithesis between *hearts*
(love) and *hands* (deeds) is natural and repeated in
Lear (I. ii. 72–73): 'It is his hand, my Lord; but I
hope his heart is not in the contents'. Othello's
passions are rising and his words are not entirely
coherent. He means 'once love and deeds went
together, but now it is all deeds (faithlessness) and
no love'.

But to know ... alms: If I know that Othello will   P. 94 LL. 2–5
not restore me to my office it will have this advantage: I shall make the best of it and try my luck elsewhere.

blank: aim, the blank being the bullseye of a target.   P. 94 L. 12

unhatch'd practice: a plot not fully matured.   P. 94 L. 26

Take ... out: copy the pattern.   P. 96 L. 4

addition: the title of honour added to the name, e.g.,   P. 96 L. 22
Lieutenant, so 'honour'.

They have it ... have it not: i.e., many are honoured   P. 97 L. 21
who have no honour.

raven ... to all: The raven was an ill-omened bird,   P. 97
foreboding disaster.   LL. 25–6

Convinced or suppli'd them: overcome them or satis-   P. 98 L. 2
fied their desires.

Lie with her ...: See note on p. 40. II. 14–31. Othello's   P. 98 L. 13
self-control is now quite broken down and he
mutters incoherent prose.

lethargy: epilepsy, as Falstaff knew – 'This apo-   P. 99 L. 1
plexy is, as I take it, a kind of lethargy'.

hurt your head?: Iago with brutal cynicism asks   P. 99 L. 8
whether Othello is not suffering from cuckold's

headache.

P. 99 L. 14   *civil*: in the double sense of 'citizen' and 'nicely behaved'.

P. 99 LL. 19–20   *nightly ... peculiar*: nightly lie in beds which they believe their own but have been shared by others.

P. 99 L. 27   *patient list*: the bounds of patience.

P. 100 L. 27   *addition*: see above p. 96 l. 22.

P. 101 L. 14   *laugh that wins*: a proverbial saying like 'he laughs best who laughs last'.

P. 103 L. 23   *patent*: formal permission.

P. 104 L. 3   *be his undertaker*: settle his business.

P. 104 L. 15   *instrument of their pleasures*: i.e., the letter which Lodovico has just delivered.

P. 105 L. 11   *Devil*: Here Othello strikes her.

P. 105 LL. 18–19   *If that the Earth ... Crocodile*: If the Earth could breed from women's tears, each tear would become a crocodile. It was an old belief that crocodiles used to cry and sob to attract the sympathetic passer-by who was then snapped up.

P. 108 L. 1   *Chuck come hither*: Othello affects to treat Desdemona as the inmate of a brothel of which Emilia is the keeper.

P. 108 L. 5   *function*: i.e., prostitution.

P. 109 LL. 6–7   *fixed figure ... finger at*: 'A perpetual mark for Scorn to point at with slowly moving finger.' A difficult image. The Quarto reads 'slow unmoving', which is preferable. *The time of Scorn*: (perhaps) Scorn for all time.

P. 109 L. 19   *quicken ... blowing*: that come to life as soon as the eggs are laid.

P. 109 L. 26   *public commoner*: one who makes herself common to all.

P. 110 L. 32   *go by water*: be expressed in tears.

P. 113 L. 2   *Comfort forswear me*: may I never have peace again. *forswear*: repudiate.

P. 114 L. 15   *You have said now*: or, in modern slang, 'sez you'.

just exception: reasonable grievance.   P. 114 L. 21

to th' vantage: 'and more too.' The *vantage* is what is P. 118 L. 29
added to exact weight.

scant ... despite: for spite cut down our allowance. P 119 L. 3

to the sense: 'to the quick.'   P. 120 L. 3

coat is better: i.e., I wear mail under my coat.   P. 120 L. 18

Enter Othello: presumably on the upper stage.   P. 120 L. 25

Minion: darling (in a bad sense).   P. 120 L. 32

No passage: no one passing.   P. 121 L. 5

So: So denotes an action, in this case the bandaging P. 122 L. 30
of Cassio's wound; later, the final killing of Desdemona (p. 128 l. 7).

monumental alablaster: an alabaster effigy. *Alablaster* P 124 L. 29
is the common Elizabethan spelling.

Promethean heat: fire from heaven. Prometheus first P. 125 L. 5
stole fire from the gods and bestowed it on man-
kind.

reprobance: damnation – by committing suicide.   P. 132 L. 25

as liberal as the North: as freely as the North wind – P. 133 L. 4
which is loud and bitter.

play the swan: i.e., will sing, for swans were sup- P. 134 L. 11
posed to break into song once only – just before
death.

sword of Spain ... temper: Spanish swords, from P. 134 L. 17
Toledo or Bilbao, were famous. *Ice-brook's temper:*
hardened in ice-cold water.

very sea-mark: A sea-mark to the mariner (like a P. 134 L. 33
land-mark to the traveller) was a conspicuous object by which he checked his course.

Man but a rush: attack him with a mere reed.   P. 135 L. 2

at compt: the Day of Reckoning.   P. 135 L 5

look ... his feet: to see whether he has cloven hoofs. P. 135 L. 21

Like the base Indian: I have kept the reading, which P. 137 L 26
is the Quarto's: the Folio reads 'Iudean'. In Elizabethan writing and printing 'J' and 'I' are the same,
and 'n' for 'u' (and vice versa) the commonest of
misprints. 'Judean' is not a Shakespearian word,

but he associates pearls with India, as in *Troilus and Cressida*, I. i. 105, (written at no great time from *Othello*): 'Her bed is India: there she lies a pearl'.

P 137 L. 30 *medicinable*: in the Quarto 'medicinal'.

P. 138 L. 10 *Spartan*: hard-hearted, for Iago views the tragedy without any sign of emotion.

P. 138 L. 15 *Let it be hid*: The bed, as is usual in Elizabethan staging, has been set up in the inner stage. At these words the curtains are closed, concealing all three bodies.

GLOSSARY

addition: title

advantage: opportunity

advocation: advocacy

affined: bound by a tie of affection

affinity: kindred

agnize: acknowledge

alteration: portentous change

amiable: loved

ancient: ensign, 2nd lieutenant

anon: directly, soon

Anthropophagi: cannibals

antres: caves

approved: proved guilty

arraigning: accusing

arrivance: arrivals, news

assay: test

atone: reconcile

attach: arrest

bauble: worthless trifle

beshrew: ill luck to

besort: proper attendants

blazoning: describing, praising

bobb'd: cheated

boding: causing foreboding

bolster: sleep together

brace: defence

bridal: wedding day

bulk: stall

butt: aim

cable: rope

caitiff: wretch

callet: drab

capable: capacious

cast: dismissed

censure: judgement

charter: privilege

check: reprimand

choler: wrath

chrysolite: jasper

circumstanc'd: put off with excuses

clip: embrace

clyster-pipes: enemas

coffers: trunks

cogging: lying

collied: made dark

coloquintida: bitter cucumber

commission: official instructions

companions: low fellows

composition: agreement

conceit: thought, idea

conceits: thinks, imagines

conception: imaginary notion

conduct: escort

conserve: distil, interpret

continuate: uninterrupted

cope: encounter

counterfeits: fakers

cozening: cheating

customer: prostitute

daff: push aside, put off

dam: mother

dear: touching closely

defeat: destroy

displeasure: lack of favour

disports: pleasures

distempering: intoxicating

doubt: suspect, suspicion
Diablo: the devil

ecstasy: violent emotion
Egyptian: gipsy
embay'd: anchored
encave: conceal
enchafed: enraged
engender'd: conceived
engluts: swallows greedily
engines: instruments of torture
ensteep'd: submerged
exhibition: allowance, reward
expectancy: hope

fadom: depth, experience
fain: gladly
favour: face
fear: frighten
fig's end: trifle
fitchew: polecat
fleers: scornful grins
flag: sign of welcome
fond: foolish
footing: arrival
fopp'd: fooled
for: because
forc'd: unnatural
forfend: forbid
fraught: freight, cargo
freeze: coarse cloth with a nap
full: complete
function: intelligence, trade
fustian: coarse cloth, nonsense

galls: tempers
gastness: terror
gender: kind
generous: noble
germans: relations

get: beget
government: self-control
grange: lonely farm
grief: suffering, pain
gripe: grip
grise: step
guardage: guardianship
gutter'd: worn into channels
gyve: fetter, ensnare

haggard: wild hawk
harlotry: harlot
hearted: heartfelt
hies: hastens
hobby-horse: low companion
housewife: hussy
humour: whim
Hydra: a many-head monster killed by Hercules

idle: waste
import: concern
incontinent: forthwith
incorporate: bodily
indign: unworthy
indirect: underhand
indues: brings to
injointed: united
ingraffed: ingrained
inhibited: prohibited
innovation: revolution
intentively: carefully

joint-ring: ring made in two pieces
jump: (1) agree; (2) exactly
just: exact

latest: last
lawn: fine linen

lay: bet, wager
learn: teach
letter: private recommendation
lown: lout

mamm'ring: hesitating
mandragora: a soporific root
match: compare
mazzard: head
medicines: love potions
mere: sheer, utter
minerals: poisonous drugs
minister: servant
moe: more
molestation: turmoil
mortal: deadly
motion: will power
mummy: concoction made from Egyptian mummies
mystery: business

nether: lower

offices: i.e., the kitchens
owe: own, possess

paddle: play lovingly
pagans: heathens
pageant: show
paragons: equals in perfection
parcels: portions
passing: exceedingly
peculiar: one's own
period: conclusion
pith: marrow
poise: counterbalance
portance: bearing
practise: plot
prefer: charge

pregnant: probable
prerogativ'd: privileged
present: immediate
prick'd: spurred
prime: eager
probal: probable
probation: proof
produced: produced as witness
profit: gain of experience
proper: (1) handsome; (2) own
propriety: natural condition
purse: draw together

qualified: mixed
qualification: allaying
quat: pimple
quicken: first have life
quillets: verbal subtleties
quirks: witty sayings, phrases

recognizance: token
remorse: (1) pity; (2) solemn obligation
repeals: recalls
reprobation: damnation
re-stem: turn back
rheum: moisture, a cold
rites: intercourse
rouse: a deep drink

salt: lustful
sans: without
'Sblood: by God's blood
scattering: casual
scored: marked as with a whip lash
secure: careless, carefree
seel: make blind
seeming: pretence

segregation: separation
self-bounty: natural goodness
sennight: week
sense: interpretation
sequent: following
sequester: separation
shrift: place for confession
Sibyl: prophetess
sith: since
skillet: saucepan
slipper: slippery
slubber: tarnish
snipe: woodcock, fool
spleen: passion of anger
stead: aid
still: always
stillness: staid behaviour
stone: turn to stone
stoup: pot holding two quarts
suppli'd: filled up

tainting: disparaging
taper: candle
teem: breed
thrice-driven: triply refined
timorous: terrifying

traverse: quick march
tupping: covering
Turk: heathen

'uds: God's
unbitted: unbridled
unbookish: simple minded
unfold: expose
unfolding: plan
unhoused: free
unlace: undo
unproper: not their own, shared

venial: pardonable
voices: votes, agreement

wage: risk
whipster: whipper-snapper
wight: creature
wrack: wreck

yerk'd: jerked, struck
yoked: married

'Zounds: by God's wounds

PENGUIN POPULAR CLASSICS

Published or forthcoming

Aesop	Aesop's Fables
Hans Andersen	Fairy Tales
Louisa May Alcott	Good Wives
	Little Women
Eleanor Atkinson	Greyfriars Bobby
Jane Austen	Emma
	Mansfield Park
	Northanger Abbey
	Persuasion
	Pride and Prejudice
	Sense and Sensibility
R. M. Ballantyne	The Coral Island
J. M. Barrie	Peter Pan
Frank L. Baum	The Wonderful Wizard of Oz
Anne Brontë	Agnes Grey
	The Tenant of Wildfell Hall
Charlotte Brontë	Jane Eyre
	The Professor
	Shirley
	Villette
Emily Brontë	Wuthering Heights
John Buchan	Greenmantle
	The Thirty-Nine Steps
Frances Hodgson Burnett	A Little Princess
	Little Lord Fauntleroy
	The Secret Garden
Samuel Butler	The Way of All Flesh
Lewis Carroll	Alice's Adventures in Wonderland
	Through the Looking Glass
Geoffrey Chaucer	The Canterbury Tales
G. K. Chesterton	Father Brown Stories
Erskine Childers	The Riddle of the Sands
John Cleland	Fanny Hill
Wilkie Collins	The Moonstone
	The Woman in White
Sir Arthur Conan Doyle	The Adventures of Sherlock Holmes
	His Last Bow
	The Hound of the Baskervilles

PENGUIN POPULAR CLASSICS

Published or forthcoming

PENGUIN POPULAR CLASSICS

Published or forthcoming